For several moments, Gabe was quiet, then felt the urge to fill that silence with words. Any words he could think of. "They actually said that I need to get back in the saddle."

"And how do you feel about that?"

"I don't even want to see a saddle."

Half of Courtney's scone was still on her plate, apparently forgotten after his confession. She met his gaze, and her own was serious. "You said on the phone that you might have a fix for the problem. Care to share?"

When Gabe had made the call, he hadn't been completely sure about this idea. Still, he'd figured reaching out couldn't hurt. In business he'd learned to go with his gut, and talking to Courtney would convince him one way or the other. They both understood family interference, and that conversation had led him to this crossroad. But he'd made up his mind when she walked into the coffee shop and unleashed those killer dimples when she smiled.

"I have a proposition for you," he started.

"Oh?" Her expression turned wary.

"You're probably going to think this is crazy. The most out-there thing you ever heard."

"Should I be afraid?" sh

"You tell me." *Here goe*
should fake date."

Dear Reader,

My husband and I were introduced by mutual friends who thought we should meet because neither of us is very tall. Successful relationships have started with less and our first contact was a phone conversation. It lasted three hours. Fortunately, we clicked face-to-face as well and fell in love. A big milestone anniversary is coming up for us this year and we owe our happily-ever-after to those matchmakers.

In *A Matchmaker's Challenge*, the hero and heroine are opposed to meeting anyone who might be a potential love interest. Courtney Davidson resists her daughter's efforts to change her mind. Love has let her down more than once and she doesn't want to be a three-time loser. But the determined teenage matchmaker with a serious romantic streak will not give up. The unrelenting campaign is driving Courtney up the wall.

Widower Gabriel Blackburne has a similar problem with his family. The corporate turnaround expert lost the woman he loved and buried the pain in work. But his family thinks he's grieved long enough and needs to get back out there. Every week at Sunday dinner there's another pretty, single woman seated next to him and he's eager to make it stop. After a chance meeting with Courtney, he comes up with a brilliant strategy that will address their shared problem—fake dating.

On paper the plan is perfect, but neither of them is prepared for the part where they fall in love.

Every relationship begins with a meet either by chance or with help. For Courtney and Gabe, it's a little bit of both. I hope you enjoy their story.

Happy reading!

Teresa Southwick

A Matchmaker's Challenge

TERESA SOUTHWICK

HARLEQUIN

SPECIAL
EDITION

If you purchased this book without a cover you should be aware
that this book is stolen property. It was reported as "unsold and
destroyed" to the publisher, and neither the author nor the
publisher has received any payment for this "stripped book."

SPECIAL EDITION™

Recycling programs
for this product may
not exist in your area.

ISBN-13: 978-1-335-89474-8

A Matchmaker's Challenge

Copyright © 2020 by Teresa Southwick

All rights reserved. No part of this book may be used or reproduced in
any manner whatsoever without written permission except in the case of
brief quotations embodied in critical articles and reviews.

This is a work of fiction. Names, characters, places and incidents
are either the product of the author's imagination or are used fictitiously.
Any resemblance to actual persons, living or dead, businesses,
companies, events or locales is entirely coincidental.

This edition published by arrangement with Harlequin Books S.A.

For questions and comments about the quality of this book,
please contact us at CustomerService@Harlequin.com.

Harlequin Enterprises ULC
22 Adelaide St. West, 40th Floor
Toronto, Ontario M5H 4E3, Canada
www.Harlequin.com

Printed in U.S.A.

Teresa Southwick lives with her husband in Las Vegas, the city that reinvents itself every day. An avid fan of romance novels, she is delighted to be living out her dream of writing for Harlequin.

Books by Teresa Southwick

Harlequin Special Edition

An Unexpected Partnership
What Makes a Father
Daughter on His Doorstep

The Bachelors of Blackwater Lake

How to Land Her Lawman
A Word with the Bachelor
Just a Little Bit Married
The New Guy in Town
His by Christmas
Just What the Cowboy Needed

Montana Mavericks: Six Brides for Six Brothers

Maverick Holiday Magic

Montana Mavericks: The Lonelyhearts Ranch

Unmasking the Maverick

Montana Mavericks: The Baby Bonanza

Her Maverick M.D.

Montana Mavericks: What Happened at the Wedding?

An Officer and a Maverick

Montana Mavericks: 20 Years in the Saddle!

From Maverick to Daddy

Visit the Author Profile page
at Harlequin.com for more titles.

This book is dedicated to all the romantics who believe in happy endings and help them along by matchmaking.

Chapter One

Courtney Davidson was late for high school, which hadn't ever happened to her even when she was a student. On top of that she was nervous—not a good look for a career-focused talk in her daughter's freshman homeroom class. The point of this whole exercise was to fire up the kids in their first year, motivate them to study hard and keep their grades up, in order to achieve every hope, dream, goal.

She planned to spotlight college and her nursing career, not the part of her own life where she got pregnant at sixteen. Sometimes it still boggled her mind that she was pushing thirty and had a kid in high school. She was trying to be someone the students looked up to, and being late wasn't what a role model was supposed to do.

After parking in the visitors' lot, Courtney ran to the designated room. In the hallway she saw two men—one fiftyish, the other in his thirties. They were standing just outside, one on either side of the door. She stopped by the younger man and leaned around him to peek inside. The teacher stood in front of the class explaining the purpose of this presentation.

"Thank goodness I'm not too late," she said to no one in particular. "I've got a minute to catch my breath." And scope out the two dads who had showed up.

The older guy in a suit and tie was standing on the far side of the doorway. He had index cards and was studying them. Courtney stood next to the other one, who was wearing tailored jeans with a white dress shirt and blazer, the walking definition of casual professional and drop-dead gorgeous. He had dark hair and a tall, lean, muscular body. His fashion vibe made her wish her scrubs were trendy instead of practical, functional and sensible.

Mr. Fashion Forward looked down at her, and crystal-blue eyes gleamed with curiosity, intelligence and a tiny bit of amusement. "Did you get hung up at work?"

His quiet, deep voice seemed to graze her skin and release tingles that touched her everywhere. She had an odd and unfamiliar urge to flirt. That was weird, because she was philosophically opposed to flirting.

"One of my patients coded," she said.

"You're a nurse."

"What gave me away?"

He shrugged. "The scrubs were a clue."

"Yeah." She glanced ruefully at her shapeless pants and top. "It's official. I get to wear pajamas to work."

"Not a bad thing." As he inspected her, his extraordinary eyes flickered with something, but it disappeared too quickly to identify. "And the patient?"

"The team got him back. He's stable. I work in the cardiac observation unit at Huntington Hills Memorial Hospital. We were prepared."

"My brother and sister work there. Mason is an ER doctor, and Kelsey is a nurse in the same department." When Courtney stared blankly, he added, "The last name is Blackburne."

She thought for a moment, then shook her head. "The name sounds familiar, but it's a big place. Doctors and staff from different departments don't overlap much."

"Seriously? You don't know everyone who works in a four-hundred-bed hospital?"

She laughed at his teasing. "I know. Slacker is my middle name. Any day I'll get a stern talking-to about that."

"As well you should."

Was he flirting? The problem with not doing it herself was that she didn't recognize the behavior in someone else.

Courtney had been half listening to the teacher inside and heard when the woman finished her opening remarks. She introduced the man with the index cards.

"Here we go." The other man smiled at them before walking inside to the front of the classroom.

Courtney had been told each of them would have ten minutes. Thank goodness she wasn't first, but she was next, and a knot tightened in her stomach.

"Are you all right?"

She looked up at the emergency room doctor's brother. "I might throw up."

"You face life-and-death situations at work all the time, and just a guess, but I bet you see blood and guts on a regular basis."

"And your point is?" she said.

"It's hard to believe public speaking makes you want to throw up."

"They're teenagers, Mr. Blackburne."

"Right. So the speech content bar isn't actually very high," he pointed out. "A healthy percentage of them are going to tune you out and possibly figure out a way to sleep sitting up. It's not personal. They're kids. And the name is Gabriel—Gabe."

"For me the bar is very high, because my daughter is in this class."

His dark eyebrows lifted in surprise. "You're not old enough to have a student in high school."

"I got an early start." This happened all the time, so her teenage humiliation had disappeared a long time ago. Now she was a proud mom. She pointed out Ava. "She's sitting in that row by the windows, in the last desk. The one with long, straight, light brown hair who's hunching down and trying to pretend she has no biological connection to me."

He laughed. "That's normal. She'll get over it."

"Easy for you to say. Or maybe not." She scanned the rows of students looking for a boy or girl with dark hair the same shade as his. "Which child is yours?"

"None of them. I don't have any children." All traces of amusement vanished as his expression hardened into an emotionless mask.

She'd hit a nerve. "I'm sorry. I didn't mean to pry. Or to assume anything."

"It's a natural assumption." The tension in his jaw eased slightly. "I was married, but my wife died."

She was momentarily shocked into silence, then said what everyone did, because "that really sucks" didn't seem appropriate. "I'm sorry."

He didn't respond at all, not even with the usual "thank you," which meant something. She just wasn't sure what. The other speaker droned on in the classroom, so she barreled ahead to fill the awkward silence. And probably made it more awkward.

"So why are you here to speak if you don't have a student in the class?" she asked. "No one does this voluntarily."

"I actually do volunteer here at the high school as a math tutor. My best friend is a teacher here at Huntington Hills High—supervisor in the department—and asked me if I could spare some time."

"And apparently you could."

"Yeah. I'm pretty good in math, and I like working with the kids. The downside is that it made me handy when someone flaked out on this career thing at the last minute." He slid his fingers into the pockets of his jeans.

"That's very nice of you. Besides being good in math, what else do you do?"

"I'm a businessman, a corporate turnaround consultant. I patch up failing companies. When your job is fixing things, you have to look at why they're broken, and I've picked up a few strategies to prevent problems before they happen."

"Right." She nodded.

"And these kids are starting their education, the part where a certain amount of pressure kicks in. Getting good grades for acceptance to top colleges. If the seeds of wisdom fall on fertile ground, their high school experience will be more successful."

"Exactly," she agreed. Lukewarm applause from the classroom trickled out into the hall. "Doesn't sound like very fertile ground in there. Tough crowd."

The unenthusiastic response made her want to throw up again. Then the fiftyish man walked out the door, looking relieved that the ordeal was over. He wished her and Gabe good luck then walked quickly toward the exit sign at the end of the hall.

"It's going to be fine," Gabe told her in a calm and reassuring tone.

"Yeah?" Courtney desperately wanted to believe him.

"I'm told after the first ten minutes you completely relax and the nerves go away."

"I only have ten minutes," she said wryly. The teacher was talking again, introducing her. "I just don't want to embarrass my daughter."

"You won't," he said confidently. "And if you do, there's always the witness protection program."

Incredibly, that made her laugh. "Seriously, Gabe, it was nice to meet you. Thanks for distracting me. If you're ever in the cardiac unit, I'll take good care of your heart."

"And who should I ask for? You never told me your name," he added.

"Courtney Davidson." Inside the classroom, the teacher said her name at almost exactly the same time. "Gotta go."

"Break a leg."

Just before she turned to leave, he gave her a thumbs-up gesture, and she smiled. Was it flirty? She hoped not and tried not to be. Ever. It could make a man think she was interested when she wasn't. She was a happily single woman trying to be the best mom possible.

And in that spirit, she gave her talk without mentioning Ava or even looking at her. She focused on the benefits of just showing up, doing the work and asking for help when, and if, you needed it. A good GPA was essential to get into the best nursing programs, and careers in the health-care field were both personally rewarding as well as a way to earn a living.

When she finished speaking, there was lively applause, which made her happy. Ava had ducked down behind the boy in front of her, so there was no way to judge her daughter's reaction. At least the other kids probably wouldn't tease her about her mom being lame and uncool. In the back of the classroom, Gabe Blackburne was clapping, too.

Courtney thanked the teacher, waved goodbye to the class and headed to the back of the room, where he was standing. "Whew, that happened."

"You were great. They loved it. No one snored, looked bored or sneaked a look at their cell phone. But, then, you look like you could be in high school yourself."

"I hope none of these kids have to grow up as fast as I did." She met his gaze. "Again, thanks for the moral support. So, I have to get back to the hospital."

"Nice to meet you, Courtney."

"Wish I could stay for your talk."

"Ask your daughter later," he suggested.

"I will. 'Bye, Gabe."

As she walked back to the parking lot, Courtney realized how very much she wanted to stay and hear what he had to say. He seemed really interesting. And she wasn't blind—there was no denying his hotness. Based on this reaction, it was probably fortunate that she had to go back to work. Saved from a potentially weak moment that she would no doubt come to regret. She'd been a two-time loser and wouldn't take a chance on third time being the charm. It could also be third strike and you're out.

Gabriel Blackburne had lost the love of his life. He wanted nothing to do with love ever again and found it painfully ironic that his current business turnaround assignment was a matchmaking company. If it hadn't been owned by his aunt, who had invested every cent of her retirement into buying Make Me a Match, he would have turned the job down flat. But Lillian Gordon was like a second mother to him.

When his own mother was on doctor-ordered bed rest during her fourth pregnancy, his aunt had stepped in and took a special and loving interest in her quiet nephew, who grew even more withdrawn during the family emergency. She'd kept him from disappearing, and he was grateful. He would do his very best to make sure that her company succeeded and she had a comfortable retirement—*if* she ever chose to stop working.

And speaking of love, it wasn't just clients finding it. His aunt's personal assistant/receptionist was flashing an engagement ring. Carla Kellerman, a petite, outspoken redhead, was in the boss's office right now showing off her rock when Gabe walked in.

"Hey, Aunt Lil. Carla, I hear congratulations are in order. Who's the lucky guy? You didn't go out with one of our clients, did you? That would violate company policy."

"Of course she wouldn't do that." His aunt was in her early sixties, and her shoulder-length hair was silver and curly. Her voice was one part gravel and two parts smoothie. "If you paid more attention, Gabriel, you would know that Carla met Steve at a bar."

"Ouch," Carla said. "That doesn't sound a whole

lot better than poaching from the client pool. However, it's essentially true. It was ladies' night at Patrick's Pub, and the rest is history."

"So romantic." Lillian sighed and leaned back in her high-back leather desk chair. "I'm a sucker for romance. Whatever it takes to bring two people together."

And that was why he'd come into her office for a chat. "Aunt Lil, you're not an amateur matchmaker setting up your friends anymore. You bought this business, and by definition that means you need to make a profit."

She smiled fondly at him. "That's why I brought you in, dear."

She wasn't wrong about that, Gabe thought. He'd come home a year ago when she called him with a 9-1-1, a business emergency. She was in financial trouble and needed his expertise. If anything about the situation was at all positive, it was the timing. He'd just completed a contract, had nothing lined up yet and looked at this interlude as a good excuse to push the pause button while he figured out what his next career move would be. But he sincerely wished his aunt was selling pork rinds instead of romance. It was hard to work up enthusiasm when he didn't believe in the product for himself. Not again.

"I am here to help, and things are heading in the right direction," he said. "But you have to stop giving away the farm."

"This is about Tanya and Jeff, I bet." Carla sighed. "They had a lovely and dreamy first date at

Le Chene. Ooh la la. Things are looking promising with those two."

"The same effect could have been achieved if we set up a lovely, dreamy meet for coffee. And far less expensive." Both women stared pityingly at him, but he wasn't budging on this. "We pay for first dates. That promotion along with our advertising and social media presence are bringing in clients and improving the revenue stream, but if you keep giving away costly first dates, there won't be a profit."

"Gabriel—"

"Don't *Gabriel* me, Aunt Lil." He rested a hip on the corner of her desk. "You brought me here to help. You asked for my expertise and advice. If you're not going to take it to heart, pun intended, I can't help you."

"Of course you're right," she said. "It's just, I do love creating an intimate and romantic setting, and that doesn't come cheap. It's hard for me to put budget over bliss and finding *the one*."

"It is pretty fantastic to meet your soul mate," Carla gushed.

Gabe knew exactly how fantastic it was. Margo had been everything to him, and he hadn't given her everything in return. There was one thing she'd wanted, and he'd put her off. Then she died, and he knew exactly how much it hurt to lose his everything. It was a once-in-a-lifetime love, and that meant no more romance for him. Unfortunately, now his job had him knee deep in romance for others to find what he would never have again.

"Why don't we research some first-date venues that are fun and lower cost?" he suggested. "The Le Chene experience could be a special promotional event to attract clients. A judiciously dangled carrot."

"Patrick's Pub is a great place," Carla said. "It fits your criteria, and I have to say, when I saw Steve, that was that. We could have been anywhere."

"Excellent idea," his aunt agreed.

"Okay."

Carla looked at her watch, then met his aunt's gaze. "Remember you said it was all right for me to leave a little early? We want a short engagement, which means flowers and vows soon. I have to shop for a wedding gown."

"Of course. Not a problem, dear." Lil waved a hand, a shooing-her-out-the-door motion, and Carla headed that way. "Gabriel and I will take care of things here."

"Thank you both." The young woman disappeared through the doorway, but her voice floated back to them. "See you in the morning."

When they were alone, he gave his aunt a look. "You're too nice. People will take advantage."

"Carla is a devoted employee because I'm a very generous boss. You catch more flies with honey than you do with vinegar, Gabriel."

"Okay." He couldn't dispute that, but he was going to watch out for her just the same. "You are in charge."

"And don't you forget it," she teased. "Oh, by the way, how did your talk at the high school go?"

"Good." Instantly an image of Courtney Davidson popped into his mind. Mom, nurse and really pretty. A favor for his friend had turned out to be more interesting than he'd expected. "The kids were polite. And asked a lot of questions." Especially Courtney's daughter.

"I'm glad to see you involved in the community. A very positive sign," his aunt said. "Would you mind manning the reception desk in Carla's absence? We don't have any appointments on the books, but just in case someone drops in, I think a Make Me a Match representative should be there. And I have some phone calls to return."

"I'm just working on spreadsheets, so doing that at her computer isn't a problem."

"Thank you, dear. In case I don't tell you enough, it means so much to me to have you here. And I'll try to restrain my romantic streak."

"No, you won't." He moved away from the desk and headed for the door. "And I wouldn't want you to. You're the heart and soul of this business, and with your personal touch and excellent instincts about people, you are going to be very successful."

"Right on, as they say." She grinned, then picked up the phone and said, "Shoo."

"And that's my cue." He left and closed her door before heading down the hall that led to the reception area.

Carla's desk was neat as a pin, thank God. He sat in front of her computer and logged on. After pulling up the files, he started to go over the monthly data, tracking revenue trends and client numbers.

It had been an adjustment working at a family-owned business. Normally his role while under contract was to advise existing management without taking an operational responsibility within the company. Here at Make Me a Match, things were different. And now he was the receptionist.

Make Me a Match occupied the top floor of a building centrally located in a Huntington Hills business park. There were two offices, a large conference area and a break room with a refrigerator and coffeepot. It was tastefully decorated with a mixture of cozy floral love seats and leather chairs. Pictures of couples walking on the beach or strolling cobblestone streets hung on the walls.

The building's elevator opened right into the reception area, and he was surprised when it stopped. Aunt Lil had said there were no appointments and drop-ins were unusual, but it seemed he was getting lucky. Contrary to what his family thought, he could be charming when he wanted to be. An opportunity to shake the rust off that skill seemed to be presenting itself.

When the doors opened, a young teenage girl got out and walked up to the desk. He recognized her from his high school talk earlier that day. She was the one who'd asked a lot of questions and pried out of him that he worked at Make Me a Match. Her mom was the pretty nurse he'd enjoyed talking to.

He knew that because Courtney had pointed her out, and she had her mom's dimples.

Gabe wasn't sure charm was part of the skill set he was going to need, though. "Can I help you?"

She was putting on a confident face, but the nerves showed. Just like her mom. "I'm here to fill out a dating profile."

"How old are you?"

"Fourteen."

That's what he'd figured. That class was all ninth graders, but asking was better than assuming. "To become a client, there's a minimum age requirement of eighteen. I'm sorry."

"Oh no," she said quickly. "It's not for me. I want to do one for my mom."

Gabe had a hard time believing the smart, funny woman he'd met earlier needed help meeting men. It had crossed his mind for a moment that in another time, another place, if he was a different person, he might have asked for her phone number or invited her for coffee. Then he remembered who he was, what had happened, and the anger kicked back in to set him straight.

"Well, Ava—"

Suspicion darkened her big brown eyes, her mom's eyes. "How do you know my name?"

Gabe was only a little surprised he remembered it. "I met your mom today when we were speaking to your class. She pointed you out."

"Oh." She slid the heavy-looking backpack off

her shoulders and rested it on the carpet. "The thing is, I want my mom to meet someone and be happy."

"Maybe she's already happy." Business 101 didn't recommend talking someone out of becoming a client. But this definitely wasn't business as usual. He glanced at the phone—one of the lines was lit, which meant he couldn't turn this girl over to his aunt. "She has you. And she's very proud of you, by the way."

"I won't be around forever. Today you said all kinds of stuff about career goals and college. I listened and plan to go. What then? She'll be all alone."

"You've got a couple of years before that. It's not something you need to worry about yet, and—"

"You don't know my mom."

True. He couldn't say it hadn't occurred to him that he might want to know her better. "Isn't this something you should discuss with her?"

"I have! She isn't easy." All the drama and angst of being a teenager was reflected in her eyes. "Finding her someone could take a while, because she's pretty stubborn. She'll be all alone and it's my fault. Because she has to take care of me."

"I'm sure she doesn't see it that way."

"That's what she says, but I don't believe her."

"You do realize that even if you fill out her profile, at some point she has to be involved in this process. If she doesn't cooperate, it's not going to work."

"I'm hoping that she'll be okay with it when she sees how much this means to me." The distress on this girl's face was almost an exact copy of her mother's when she'd warned that she might throw up. "If you're worried about your fee, don't be. I've saved up money from my allowance and babysitting."

She was killing him. "Look, Ava, because you're underage, taking you on as a client is walking a very fine ethical line on company policy."

"You have to help me." Frustration wrapped around every word. "This company stands by its commitment to make meeting someone easier. I know that because I checked you out on the internet."

The internet was a blessing and a curse. Gabe had a bad feeling that if he didn't do something, there were a lot of bad places it could take this kid. And Ava, with her saved-up babysitting money, really got to him. So he made a snap decision.

"Okay. I'll put together some paperwork for you to fill out. Contact information for your mom, a questionnaire about her likes and dislikes. That sort of thing. We'll get some notes and go from there to get her on board with this whole idea." He pulled open one of Carla's lateral file drawers and pulled out a sheet of paper, then indicated one of two chairs in front of the desk. "Have a seat and we'll get this rolling."

"Thank you, Mr. Blackburne." She sat down, took the pen he held out and started filling in the information.

The hopeful look on her face followed by relief when he relented made him feel like slime for deceiving her. He would get Courtney's phone number from the contact sheet, then let her know what was going on. He was in over his head and eager to pass this on to a parent.

When Ava had completed it, he took the single sheet and handed her a clipboard with several more attached. "The questions are general, designed to create a profile to generate interest. But that shouldn't be a problem. You seem to know your mom pretty well. Do the best you can with the answers."

"Okay." She smiled. "Thanks."

Please don't thank me, he thought. "Can I get you something to drink? Coffee, water, soda?"

"A soda, maybe," she said hesitantly.

"Okay. You start working on that and I'll go get it."

"Okay." She nodded then bent her head and concentrated on the paperwork in her lap.

Gabe took the single sheet with him to the break room and pulled out his cell phone then punched Courtney's number into the keypad. She was probably dealing with a coding patient or something, but he could leave a voice mail with bullet points of the situation along with his heartfelt appeal for her to call him back ASAP.

"Hello?" A familiar female voice answered on the fourth ring.

"Courtney?"

"Yes. Who is this?"

"Gabe Blackburne. We met today at the high school."

"I remember." There was a pleasantly surprised

note in her tone before it changed when she asked, "How did you get my number?"

Bullet points, he reminded himself. "I work at a company called Make Me a Match. Ava is here to fill out a dating profile for you. She's determined that you meet someone."

"I'm sorry, what?"

"Your daughter is in my office doing paperwork right now. I thought you should know." There was no reason she should believe him, so he added, "This isn't a joke. And if you want a character reference for me, call Brett Kamp at the school. I promise you this is for real and I'm just trying to help."

There was a brief hesitation on the other end of the line, as if she was weighing his words. Finally she said, "Okay. Thank you. If you'll give me your office address, I'll come right over and get her."

"Of course. I'll text it to you."

"Fine. This must be an awful inconvenience for you. I'm very sorry." Then she hung up.

Gabe wasn't sorry. And that was a surprise. Courtney Davidson had raised an independent and caring young woman who would go the extra mile to see her mom happy. That intrigued him and, against the odds, he was looking forward to seeing her again.

Chapter Two

She could be more humiliated, but Courtney wasn't sure how. Ava had told Gabriel Blackburne that her mother couldn't get a man without help. She could easily get one, thank you very much. She just didn't *want* one.

After letting the nursing supervisor know she had an emergency and was leaving for a short while, she drove to the address Gabe had texted her. It turned out that his office building wasn't far from the hospital. She pulled into the lot, found a parking space, then jumped out of the car and ran into the lobby. After searching the directory, she found Make Me a Match on the top floor.

She pushed the up button and waited impatiently

for the elevator to arrive. "Come on. Come on," she pleaded.

Finally the doors opened and a couple of people exited. She got in and punched the floor button as if she had a personal grudge against it. That could happen, since the thing moved like a snail. It was a misguided illusion to make the ride go faster, but she ticked off every floor anyway, praying the thing wouldn't stop for someone to get on. At long last the top floor arrived, and the doors opened onto the reception area for Make Me a Match.

The spacious room was empty except for Gabe Blackburne, just as handsome as he'd been earlier that day. To notice a thing like that at a time like this meant she had to be going a little crazy.

"Where's Ava?" She rushed over to him, and he came around the desk to meet her.

"She's in my aunt's office filling out your dating profile." There must have been a horrified look on her face, because he added, "Don't worry. I'll take care of destroying whatever paperwork she's filling out."

"It's not that. I'm concerned about my daughter."

"She's fine."

"Of course she's not fine. She's supposed to be at her friend's house doing homework, but she's here. Matchmaking for her mother. There's nothing remotely fine about that. It's wrong in so many ways." Strands of hair had come loose from the clip she used to pull it back, and she tucked them behind her ears. Her hands were shaking. "Which way to your aunt's office? I'll just get my little delinquent and be out of your way."

"There's no rush," Gabe said.

"No rush?" Courtney couldn't decide whether his calm manner was more soothing or annoying. "There's definitely a rush. Not only do I hope the quicker I do that, the quicker you'll forget she was here, but I can't wait to ground her for the rest of her life."

"Maybe you should take a deep breath first." He half sat on the edge of the reception desk and folded his arms over an impressive chest. "Have a seat. Count to ten."

Courtney wasn't sure why, but she sat in one of the two barrel-back chairs. "I can't believe you actually let her fill out a dating profile for me."

"I was stalling for time. If she was turned away, I was afraid she would resort to the internet, and there are so many places there she shouldn't go."

"Oh God—" Her mouth trembled for a moment, and she covered it with her hand. "I had no idea she was that determined."

"She saved up her babysitting money to pay the agency fee," he said kindly. "Obviously she loves you very much."

To her horror, Courtney's eyes filled with tears. There was a box of tissues on the desk, and Gabe grabbed one, then handed it to her.

"I need to thank Carla tomorrow," he mumbled.

"Ava can be a headstrong brat, but she means everything to me." She met his sympathetic gaze, and something broke loose inside her, like a chunk of ice off a glacier. "I was pregnant at sixteen, and when she was born, my parents kicked me out because I couldn't give her up for adoption like they wanted me to. They said it was my problem and I could just solve it on my own."

"What about the father?" Gabe's jaw hardened, and his eyes smoldered with what looked like anger.

"He was older and just disappeared. I was on my own." She swiped away the single tear that rolled down her cheek and squeezed the tissue into her fist. "One of the hospital nurses had a spare room and took us in. I finished high school online and worked part-time. That extraordinary woman made me want to be a nurse."

"And you are."

"I could finally provide for us, give her a life. But I wanted her to have a traditional upbringing. White picket fence and two parents. After her bio-dad disappeared, I wasn't inclined to trust men, but I met one and made an exception. Thought I was in love. Married him. Found out he was a jerk. Divorced him." She got up and started pacing. "And why am I telling you all this?"

"I have a sympathetic face?" he offered.

"No. Well, yes, you do. But this isn't me. It's been a terrible day. I lost a patient. Crisis after crisis. I didn't have lunch because of speaking at the high school." Helplessly, she looked at him. "I don't do this. We just met. You must think I'm a nutcase."

"No. But I have a sneaking suspicion your low

blood sugar might be responsible." He straightened away from the desk and took her hand. "Come with me."

"No. Gabe—" She tried to stop and pull her hand free, but he was strong and seemed determined to lead her down the hall. "I have to get Ava out of here."

He didn't respond, just took her into a small room with a card table, a few cupboards, a coffeepot on the granite countertop and a refrigerator. After pulling out one of the chairs, he gently nudged her to sit in it.

"First you're going to have something to drink and a snack."

Courtney was suddenly too drained to rebel and simply let out a long sigh. In a few moments he set a small paper plate in front of her containing cheese and apple slices. Then he got a glass and filled it with ice and a clear soda.

"Eat, drink," he ordered.

"It's a good thing you didn't say 'and be merry,' because I think that's too much to ask." She ate a piece of cheese followed by some apple and privately thought it was more delicious than anything she'd ever tasted before.

It was psychological, because her body couldn't possibly have time to process the food so fast, but she started to feel a lot better. Gabe sat across from her and watched silently as the snack quickly disappeared.

When it was gone, he said, "Do you want more?"

"No, thank you. That was perfect. And delicious. Perfectly delicious."

Amusement pierced his air of seriousness for a moment, then was gone. "Feel better?"

She nodded. "Except for being embarrassed. I can't imagine what you must think."

"Only that I hope you're feeling better."

"Physically, yes. Emotionally? I'm on the edge." She sighed. "I feel as if I owe you an explanation."

"I'm not asking for one," he assured her.

"Still…" She took a deep breath. "Ava has been pushing me to date. I'm opposed to the idea for reasons you can probably figure out from what I shared with you. But she needs to stand down."

"In her defense, I have to say she's concerned about you being all by yourself when she goes to college." He looked down for a moment, as if he was weighing something. "And she blames herself for you being alone."

"I've told her that isn't the case," Courtney protested. "That I'll be fine. I'm really okay and she doesn't need to worry."

"All evidence to the contrary," he said wryly.

"Right. Because she's here. Filling out a dating profile." She thought about that for a moment. "I'm not sure how she thought I'd be involved with the agency."

"She was hoping when you saw how much it means to her that you'd get on board with the process."

Wow, Ava had really confided a lot to him. Come

to think of it, Courtney had, too. Like mother, like daughter. Why stop now?

"Look, Ava is a romantic. And she's a nag." Her energy level was rising. Courtney could tell by the way her inner flirt was beginning to stir to life. Her plan was to ignore it. "All those fairy tales and happily-ever-after cartoons that end with a kiss are to blame. I have absolutely no desire to find a man or look for love. My problem is that I don't know how to make her stop pushing me without crushing the sense of romance out of her."

"It appears she doesn't understand the meaning of the word *no*," he pointed out.

"Yeah, there's that. Plus, I don't want to limit her in any way. She might have better luck than me and find the love of her life. Be deliriously happy." She met his gaze. "I see my job as her mom to encourage her to experience things. I don't want to be only a horrible warning, someone who makes her not want to try."

"I see your dilemma."

"Any suggestions?" she asked.

"Go on a date." He shrugged. "Go through the motions."

"Even if I wanted to, it's just not that easy." She sipped the soda. "But you're a man. I don't expect you to understand."

"I'm not sure what that means. No doubt that's because I haven't done much dating since my wife died."

Courtney barely held back a wince. She'd forgotten about that and could have kicked herself for being so insensitive. "I didn't mean to insult you. It's just that I'm a woman with a daughter. Nine times out of ten, a man is going to pick someone without baggage or responsibilities. I have both."

His blue eyes narrowed as he looked at her. "Is it possible you're selling men short?"

"That's the thing. I don't have the energy or the inclination to find out."

"Ava said you weren't easy. I can see what she was talking about."

What? Courtney was a little peeved that her own child had warned this man, of all men, about her mother's stubborn streak. Ava was right, but still. Part of her cared what he thought, and she didn't want difficult or needy to be the first character traits that popped into his mind when he thought of her. *If* he thought of her. He probably couldn't wait for her to leave and never darken his doorway again.

Before she could respond, voices in the hall drifted to her, and then the hooligan in question came into the break room with an older woman. The four of them stared at each other for several moments.

"I'm Lillian Gordon, Gabriel's aunt," the woman said. "You must be Ava's mother."

"Guilty." Courtney stood and shook the woman's hand. Then she met her daughter's sheepish gaze. "I need to apologize for my daughter disrupting your office, Mrs. Gordon."

"It's Lillian. And Ava didn't interrupt anything. She's delightful."

"She is many good and wonderful things," Courtney said. "Right now delightful isn't one of them."

"Try not to be too hard on her." Gabe stood.

"You should listen to him, Mom." Ava caught her look and wisely stopped there.

"Remember, she has your best interests at heart," he added.

And by that he meant she blamed herself for Courtney being alone. She was going to have to find a way to get Ava over that hang-up, but it was a challenge for another time.

Courtney smiled tightly at Lillian then looked at him. "I need to take Ava home and get back to work. Please know how very much I appreciate your phone call and concern for my daughter. I'll do my level best to make sure she doesn't bother you again."

"It was no bother." Gabe looked completely sincere.

Still, Courtney figured that was just him being polite. He was a business guy who fixed financially troubled companies. It was a logical assumption that Make Me a Match was in trouble. Therefore he wouldn't ever give a potential customer any reason not to come back. Even though she'd assured him the service provided was the last thing she wanted.

Gabe walked them to the elevator. Courtney was a sucker for gentlemanly gestures, and this qualified big-time.

When the doors opened, he said, "It was a pleasure to meet you both. And I really mean that."

Ava gave him a scathing look, one that Courtney knew all too well. "I can't believe you ratted me out."

The teen's scornful glance didn't seem to faze him. "Sorry, kid. You don't get it now, but it was the right thing to do."

"It was," Courtney agreed. "Thank you again. For everything."

The two of them got into the elevator, and when the doors closed, she felt oddly deflated. Her inner flirt wasn't too happy, either. It was a good thing that there was no reason to come back.

Every Sunday Gabe's mother cooked a big dinner, and all of her children were expected to show up unless there was a very good excuse. Like being on another planet. Since he was back in Huntington Hills, there was no acceptable reason to be absent, so here he was driving up to the house. After a count of the cars out front, it was clear that he was the last to arrive.

For a moment he sat and looked at the lush green grass and neatly trimmed bushes in front of the place where he'd grown up. Memories scrolled through his mind. Playing football on the lawn. Riding bikes and skateboarding on the sidewalk. The scary weeks that seemed like forever when his mom was put on bed rest because of a high-risk pregnancy and he thought she was going to die.

Aunt Lil had seen how scared Gabe had been and spent a lot of time with him, trying to ease his fears. Ever since she had been protective of him, and they were very close. He recalled bringing girls home to meet the family. After he first introduced them to Margo, his mother told him she knew this was *the one* because of the way he looked at her. Margo had been gone over two years now, and he was just as angry about losing her.

He turned off the car's engine and exited, then headed to the front door and opened it. Instantly he was hit with the noise and chaos always generated by this big, close-knit family.

Flo Blackburne spotted him right away, as if she'd been watching for him. Her blond hair was short and her energy boundless. She met him in the entryway and threw her arms around him. "Hi, you."

"How are you, Mom?"

"Happy," she said. "All my children and grand-children are here. The whole family together. It doesn't get any better than this."

Gabe nodded as he scanned the family room full of Blackburnes. His oldest brother, Mason, was there with his pregnant wife, Annie. Their two-year-old twins, Sarah and Charlie, were squealing with de-light as his brother, Dominic, tickled, teased and let them climb all over him on the family room floor. Kelsey was in the kitchen stirring something on the stove—gravy, judging by the large roast on the plat-ter beside her.

His dad, John, was chatting with a pretty young brunette Gabe had never seen before, and he glanced down at his mother. "Who's Dad talking to?"

"Oh, that's Ember." There was a very deliberate and fake note of innocence in her voice.

"Why is she here?"

"She's new to the area and doesn't know many people." She smiled and shrugged. "You know me. Always taking in strays."

"Is it a coincidence that all the strays you take in are attractive women? And this is the fourth or fifth time."

"Really?" Again with the innocence. "I hadn't noticed."

"Uh-huh." He sent her a warning look. "Will it be a coincidence when she sits next to me at dinner?"

"Everyone sits where they want to, Gabe. You know that." But there was a look in her eyes. "Now go mingle. And be friendly."

"I always am."

But by friendly she meant introduce himself to the newcomer, and he managed to avoid that. Call him rebellious or spiteful. Either worked.

He chatted with Mason and played with the kids, trying in vain to tamp down envy of his brother's family—a beautiful wife and two children with another on the way. After exchanging small talk, Annie excitedly grabbed his hand and put it on her pregnant belly so he could feel the baby move. That was pretty awesome. Then he headed to the isolation of the kitchen—some might call it hiding. But his sister was there putting the final touches on dinner.

"How's it going, sis?"

Kelsey looked up from the mashed potatoes she was stirring. "It's good."

He leaned against the counter and folded his arms over his chest. "What's new?"

"Not much." Her dark blond hair was pulled into a knot on the top of her head. Big blue eyes met his. "You?"

"Same old," he answered.

"How's business?"

"We're getting there. The client base is growing." He thought about Courtney, although technically she wasn't a client.

"What?" Kelsey was staring at him.

"Hmm?"

"You were smiling just now. You don't smile much. A scowl or glare is more your style. So I'd like to know what produced a rare happy expression on your face."

"Oh. I had a client the other day who dropped in."

"And?" Kelsey prompted.

"She's fourteen."

His sister's eyes widened. "Didn't know Aunt Lil was catering to young adults."

"She's not. That would violate company policy. The kid was there to help her mom find a man so when she goes off to college her mother won't be alone."

"Oh my gosh." Kelsey had that mushy look on her face that women often got. "That's so sweet."

"As I said, also too young for the service we provide."

"So what did you do?"

"I called her mother." He remembered that his sister worked at the same hospital. "She's a cardiac care nurse. Do you know Courtney Davidson?"

She thought for a moment. "I think I've seen her in the cafeteria. Pretty brunette with brown eyes and adorable dimples."

"Yeah."

"She has a teenage daughter?" Her eyes widened in disbelief.

"Early start, apparently. Great kid, too," he added.

"She sounds very independent and thoughtful. And you tattled on her."

"That's what she said." He crossed his feet at the ankles. "I didn't want her turning to the internet."

"I see your point." Kelsey lowered the heat under the big pot of potatoes. "Dinner's ready."

That announcement caused another level of chaos at the Blackburne house. The meal was served buffet style, so everyone fell into line, and somehow Gabe ended up last. His mother was in the dining room directing traffic. By the time he got there, the only chair left was next to Ember. *Coincidence my ass*, he thought.

Enough already.

But the young woman smiled sweetly. "We haven't met yet. I'm Ember Kiley."

"Gabriel Blackburne."

"I met your mom at the dermatology office where she works. The next thing I knew, I had an invitation to Sunday dinner."

"Yeah. That's my mom." He glanced at the other end of the table, where Aunt Lil sat with her sister in life and in matchmaking. They huddled together, coconspirators, watching him and trying not to be obvious about it. *They should never give up their day jobs for undercover work*, he thought.

"I recently moved here from Indiana. I'm working for a temp agency and trying to break into modeling. The doctor your mom works for is helping clear up my skin."

"I see." Her skin looked perfectly fine to him, and there was nothing wrong with her goals. It just wasn't nursing or raising a teenage girl.

He'd thought about Courtney a lot since that day at Make Me a Match. Probably because he respected the hell out of her—no offense to Ember. It wasn't her fault she was being used. And that had to stop.

Dinner felt endless, and if not for his brother's two-year-old son, Charlie, who sat beside him, Gabe would have been bored out of his mind. The little guy rubbed mashed potatoes and gravy in his hair then started chucking peas. Annie was equal parts horrified and mortified by her child. Mason predicted his son would someday pitch for a major league baseball team. Gabe blessed the boy for a much-needed distraction. And finally the evening came to an end.

Everyone said their goodbyes, and Ember was the last to leave. She asked for his phone and put her number in it, then smiled and left. Gabe loitered a little longer, and when his father and sister were watching a movie in the family room, he walked into the kitchen. Aunt Lil and his mom were there putting away leftovers and washing pots and pans.

It was time to give them a piece of his mind about their matchmaking. He cleared his throat. "It's like I'm psychic, Mom. I ended up sitting next to the single, attractive woman even though Dom is available, too."

"Ember is very pretty and sweet, don't you think?" His mother was drying the meat platter with a dish towel.

"Very pretty," he agreed. "And I'm not interested."

"Did you even give her a chance, Gabriel?" Aunt Lil rinsed a soapy copper-bottom saucepan and handed it to her sister.

"I was friendly as I would be to anyone who was a guest in your home."

"It seemed to me that you paid more attention to Charlie than you did to her." There was the tiniest bit of censure in his mother's tone. "That little sweetheart doesn't need encouragement to be naughty, and when you pay attention to that behavior…"

He hated it when she looked disappointed in him, and that put him on the defensive. "That kid is something else. He really played to his audience."

"You really shouldn't encourage him, dear." But Aunt Lil grinned. "I remember when you used to wear your food like that."

"If only we'd had cell phone cameras and Facebook. The toddler years would be around to humble you forever. But fortunately you outgrew that stage." His mom set the clean, dry saucepan on the stove.

"I saw Ember give you her number. Are you going to call her?"

"I didn't ask for it. And, no, I'm not going to get in touch."

"Why?" Aunt Lil asked, but both women stared questioningly at him.

They were in cahoots. Apparently both had the matchmaking gene and were using it enthusiastically on him, trying to fix him. But that wasn't going to happen. His heart was shattered into pieces, and so many were missing, putting it back together again would be impossible.

"Look, I know you love me. And your intentions are good. But stop throwing women at me." He blew out a breath in frustration. "It's awkward and not fair to them."

"Oh, Gabe, you need to make an effort. It's way past time for you to get back in the saddle."

"No, Mom." Anger churned inside him. Since Margo had died, that emotion had been his constant companion, a shield against more complex feelings he ignored. "I'm not interested. You have to stop. Please."

Was that begging? It sounded a lot like desperate begging to him.

"Lillian, can you talk to your nephew? You're the one who could always get through to him. I'm only his mother."

"Mom, come on—"

"No." She tossed down the dish towel. "You have no idea how hard it is for a mother to watch her child hurting and not be able to help. Especially when he won't help himself."

"It's not that I don't appreciate what you're trying to do."

"When you have children you'll understand." She walked over to him and put a hand on his cheek, then smiled sadly and walked out of the room.

She loved him. Gabe was keenly aware of that. She also knew him better than anyone except Aunt Lil, which was why those particular words opened a pocket of guilt and sent it pouring through him. Because he was selfish and had wanted a little more time for his career before having a child, Margo never got what she wanted most—to be a mother. If they'd had a baby, he would still have a part of her with him. Being alone was his punishment to bear.

He looked at his aunt. "I'm not trying to be difficult."

"Neither are we." She let the water out of the sink. "It's just when you love someone, you worry about them. And you know what they say about stress and worry." She waited a beat and filled in the blank. "It can take years off your life."

Great. Just what he needed. More guilt.

The last thing he wanted was for his family to worry, but love? It wasn't for him. No way. So, rock, meet hard place. What the hell was he supposed to do? He had no desire to go down the dating road again.

He remembered glibly saying that to Courtney Davidson when she was venting about her daughter pushing her to meet someone. His flippant suggestion had been to date. Go through the motions. He was in the same predicament with his family—and suddenly the idea light switched on.

Chapter Three

The downside of grounding your teenager was being cooped up with said teen. Ava had taken the bus to a place she wasn't supposed to be. *And* she'd lied about being at a friend's house. Courtney thought a week for each offense was fair, but seven days later she was starting to rethink that decision. This wasn't about going soft or the enforced proximity with a hormonal fourteen-year-old girl. But when she got home from work and found a note on her laptop listing five reasons Ava should be ungrounded, doubts started to creep in.

Courtney felt a tightness in her chest at the salutation. Ava rarely called her *Mommy* anymore. When she did, everything inside her melted.

Dear Mommy,
I hope you will read this with an open mind,
because I think you are being totally unfair. It's
not like I was drinking or doing drugs.
1) You don't know what I'm going through. My
social life will never recover. I'll never have a
boyfriend because you're too strict.
2) I'll call you gorgeous and the best mom ever
in the world for a whole month.
3) First-time felon should get leniency.
4) I've learned my lesson in only a week.
5) I promise to work harder in math and bring
up my grade.
Love,
Your daughter, Ava

It was time for a mother-daughter chat. Courtney was an optimist and believed there was a chance that if she explained her reasons, her daughter would understand why she had to stick to her guns. There would be no commuting her sentence.

She set the pizza she'd brought home on the granite-topped kitchen counter and walked upstairs to Ava's room. Courtney loved her town house, partly because it was hers and she'd bought it by herself. But it was also open and cute and suited them perfectly. The downstairs consisted of kitchen, dining, living and family rooms.

There were three bedrooms on the second floor, and as she walked up, she smiled at the hanging framed photos of Ava from infancy to middle school graduation. This girl was her life, and she never felt as if she was a good enough mom. If she'd done a better job, maybe Ava wouldn't have lied. Should she ground herself for being a bad mother?

That train of thought was unproductive.

She stopped in front of the first door at the top of the stairs and took a deep breath before knocking. "Ava?"

"Come in."

Courtney did and braced herself for the chaotic mess her girl seemed to prefer to neat and tidy. It was a surprise when neat and tidy greeted her. The light beige carpet was visible because no clothes littered the floor. White shelves were organized, and childhood books straightened and dusted. The plum-and-green floral comforter was neatly pulled up to cover the sheets and blanket on the full-size bed. Schoolbooks were open along with Ava's laptop. The teen was sprawled out on her belly, fingers poised over the keys as if she'd been doing homework.

"Your room looks so organized. A place for everything and everything in its place."

"It's not like I have anything else to do." There was only a small amount of bitterness in her tone. Apparently Ava recognized it and instantly smiled brightly. "You're home. How was your day?"

"Not bad." She held up the note. "This is impressive. But, I gotta say, it could backfire on you. Because you're really using this time productively. Your room is spotless and homework is done without a fight. And the part about never having a boyfriend doesn't break my heart. Your grounding is working for me in a very big way."

"Seriously, Mom—" She sat up in the middle of the bed. "I'm not going to get pregnant like you did."

Courtney hoped not. She hadn't been much older than Ava when it happened to her, and she'd been forced to grow up way too fast. That's not what she wanted for her daughter. Oh, how she wished for the terrible twos back. She couldn't wait for that stage to pass, but she'd take it over this teen stuff in a heartbeat.

But she'd always tried to be open and honest about everything. "I can't help worrying about it, Ava."

"I promise I won't make the same mistake."

"Oh, sweetie—" Courtney walked over to the bed and sat on the edge. "You're not a mistake."

"I sure wasn't planned."

"You're not wrong about that, but it doesn't make you a mistake." She tucked a silky brown strand of hair behind her daughter's ear. Gabe had said that Ava blamed herself for Courtney being alone. How could she convince this amazing girl that wasn't true? What combination of words would get through to her? Like she used to do when Ava was small, she ran her finger over a soft cheek then lightly tapped her turned-up nose. "You are the best thing that ever happened to me."

"Then unground me."

"I have to admit that you make a compelling case. Especially number two—gorgeous mom—and number five, working harder on math. Those two are my favorites, and I'm tempted."

"Then go for it." Ava looked hopeful and pathetic at the same time.

"Sweetie, I have to make a point here. What you did was dangerous."

"No, it wasn't. Mr. Blackburne is a really cool guy. I knew that because I talked to him at school that day."

"Yes, he seems nice." Courtney had met him, too, and fought the flirty feeling. He reminded her of the guy in high school, the cute and funny boy who made you eager to go to class every day. Then to have her daughter show up at his office to get help finding a man for her? That was awkward, uncomfortable and embarrassing. Not to mention worrisome. "What if you'd been wrong about him being a nice man?"

"I wasn't."

This was getting her nowhere. Maybe another perspective would help. "Did it occur to you that I was embarrassed?"

"Why?"

"Because my child involved strangers in my personal life in a way that was less than flattering."

"I don't see how." Ava shrugged dismissively as only a fourteen-year-old could.

"Okay. Let's see if I can explain this." She thought for a moment. "Imagine you had a crush on the most popular boy in school—"

"Nick Perino." Ava's eyes took on a dreamy expression.

So, that didn't take her long, Courtney thought. "You have a crush on Nick and you're talking to him at lunch. In the crowded cafeteria. You're standing and drop something. You bend over to pick it up, and your jeans split open."

Dreamy eyes suddenly went wide in horror. "Oh my God—"

"You see where I'm going with this?" Courtney felt as if she was getting somewhere. To bring her point home, she said, "It would be so mortifying. You might never want to show your face at school again."

"So, you have a crush on Mr. Blackburne."

"What? No. I was just trying to explain how awful I felt because of what you did."

"But it's like you said," Ava told her. "You don't have to see him again."

Courtney actually wouldn't have minded seeing Gabe again, but now that he knew what a romantic loser she was, he would probably rather poke a sharp stick in his eye than be caught talking to her. And she knew this child was bright enough to get the concept. This dense stubbornness was a facade. It was time to get tough. "The second and arguably most important reason you're grounded is because you lied to me. You were not where you told me you would be."

"It was a lie of good intentions," Ava defended.

"But sooner or later I was going to find out what you did. That never occurred to you?"

"By then I figured you'd be excited about going on a date."

"That backfired on you big-time, didn't it?" In her mind, Courtney was beating her head against the wall and hoped it didn't show on the outside. She counted to ten slowly, then said, "It turns out that dating isn't as important to me as making sure my child grows up to be honest and truthful."

Ava huffed out a breath. "Mom, what do you have against dating?"

"It's not going out that I have a problem with." *It's going out with irresponsible, lying, weasel-dog men*, she thought. But saying that out loud would put her squarely into crushing-romantic-dreams territory.

"Okay, then," Ava cried. "So you will go out on a date."

"That's not what I said."

"Come on, Mom. Just one date and I'll quit bugging you for a month."

"Tempting."

Ava's eyes lit up. "If you actually get a boyfriend, I'll back off for an entire year."

"Can I get that in writing?"

Her daughter pulled a notebook from the backpack on the bed beside her, opened it and started to write. Out loud she said, "I, Ava Davidson, do solemnly promise that if Courtney Davidson, my mother, goes out on a date, I will—"

"Stop. I was joking."

"This isn't funny, Mom. My social future is at stake."

"I thought this was about me being happy."

"It is. But we could both be happy at the same

time. Wouldn't that be good?" Ava could be as charming and sweet and funny as she was pouty and brooding and persistent.

Courtney knew that a bratty attitude was just one negative answer away. She'd had a long day at work and was tired and hungry. Now she could add frustrated to the list, and her reserves of patience were used up.

"Nice try, kiddo. But you're still grounded. For another week."

"But—"

"Keep it up," Courtney warned, "and there will be an essay added to your sentence. The topic will be why lying to your mother is wrong." She held up a finger to forestall any pushback when Ava opened her mouth. "Not another word."

Before Ava could test her yet again, Courtney walked to the door. "I brought home a pizza. I'll make a salad to go with it."

"I'm not hungry."

"Suit yourself."

A sulking teenager who gave her the drop-dead-bitch look. Yup, Courtney thought sarcastically, she was hands-down the best mom ever.

In the kitchen, she deleted the five reasons to be ungrounded note and closed her laptop. Then she pulled salad makings from the refrigerator. Carrots, cucumber, avocado and lettuce wouldn't make her feel as good as kettle chips and cookies, but veggies had a lot fewer calories. Taking the nutritional high road would have to be enough.

She'd just finished tossing the salad with balsamic vinegar and olive oil when her cell phone rang. A robocalling telemarketer was just what she needed to make her deteriorating mood complete. Blocking the number would give her great pleasure, but she had to make sure this was someone she never wanted to talk to again.

"Hello."

"Courtney?" A man's voice.

"Yes," she said suspiciously. "Who's this?"

"Gabe Blackburne." There was a hesitation. "Are you okay? You sound really ticked off."

"Sorry. It was one of those days." Why did every interaction with him seem to happen on one of those days? But just hearing his deep, warm, melted-chocolate voice punctured her bitterness balloon and let all the anger out. On top of that, her heart actually skipped a beat. As a cardiac nurse, she should know.

"How are you?" he asked.

"Good. But, I have to admit, a little surprised to hear from you."

"Yeah. There's something I'd like to run by you. Are you busy right now?"

"Not if you don't count negotiations with a grounded teenager who doesn't understand the meaning of the word *no*."

He laughed. "Ava is giving you a hard time?"

Courtney looked at the crumpled note in the trash and sighed. "Let's just say she could have a future as an attorney. Making an argument is what she does best."

"Oh?"

"On top of bargaining for a reduced sentence for lying to me, she's still on my case about dating. Relentless is her middle name."

"I see." There was another pause. "As it happens, I just might have a fix for the problem."

"Really?"

"Can you meet me for coffee?"

If he had a solution that would stop the insane harassment, he could definitely count her interested. "I can do that. As long as this isn't a date."

"Heaven forbid."

"Okay then."

They agreed on a time and place, and Courtney hung up. She stared at her cell phone for a few moments. That was completely unexpected. And she was equal parts excited to see him again and curious about what he had to say. She was tempted to change out of her scrubs but didn't. Feeling flirty was one thing. Acting on it was a road she didn't want to go down.

For his meet with Courtney, Gabe chose a little shop not far from the hospital. Coffee Break wasn't one of those commercialized franchise places but a cozy, independently owned business. The walls were decorated with a mural of coffeepots and steaming cups. Booths lined the wall across from the dessert case, and circular tables filled the center of the room. It was crowded in spite of the fact that it was dinnertime for most people, and a lot of the customers were wearing scrubs, a clue that they worked at the hospital.

He picked a booth and sat facing the door so he could see Courtney when she arrived. Since it was dinnertime he'd suggested meeting a little later, but she insisted a break from her hostile first-time felon was just what she needed. Would she still feel that way after he pitched his proposal?

When he called, she'd sounded pleased to hear from him, but that could change when he told her what he had in mind.

A teenage server came over. Her name tag said Toni.

"Welcome to Coffee Break. What can I get you?"

"I'm waiting for someone," he said. "Can you come back when she gets here?"

"Sure thing."

He folded his hands on the table and settled in to wait, wondering if she would actually show or stand him up. The idea of her not coming made him realize that he was actually looking forward to seeing her again. That thought had barely crossed his mind before she walked in, still wearing her scrubs from work. Courtney looked around, obviously not seeing him at first, and frowned. When she spotted him, she smiled, a look that transformed her from pretty to beautiful. She had killer dimples. Really killer.

It wasn't that he hadn't noticed them, first when they met and again in his office, but somehow he'd overlooked this fact. He hadn't felt awareness of any woman for a long time, even though there were attractive women at his mother's house on a regular basis. But there he shut down, and that had rusted out his ability to recognize this for what it was. Courtney was different. She was interesting.

She walked over to the booth and slid in across from him. "Hi."

"Thanks for coming. Hope this place is okay. I figured you would know it."

"You figured right." She settled her purse beside her on the bench seat. "The hospital cafeteria is handy, and the food's not bad. But sometimes you just need to get out and clear your head. This place is just what the doctor ordered."

"No pun," he teased.

"Right." Her dimples flashed when she smiled. "And, frankly, I owe you one. You rescued me from a very hostile environment."

Before he could ask for details about what was going on, Toni, the server, walked over. "Everyone here now?"

"Yes." He looked at Courtney. "What would you like?"

"Caramel and vanilla latte. Decaf. And a petite pumpkin scone."

"Black coffee for me," Gabe said.

"Nothing sweet to go with that?" Toni asked.

"No. I think that will do it."

"Coming right up." She walked away.

"Did you have dinner?" he asked Courtney.

"I brought home a pizza, which I hoped would buy me some goodwill with my incarcerated teenager."

"And?" he prompted.

"Not so much." She sighed. "I found a note on my computer listing five reasons I should reverse her sentence."

"That's pretty inventive." He laughed. "Did the strategy work?"

"Absolutely not. Showing any sign of weakness would give her the upper hand." She met his gaze. "Ava might not understand completely why I'm being so tough on her about this particular infraction, but what she did could have been dangerous. You saw that right away. Compliments to you on getting it, by the way."

"It's not about knowing kids. I'm trying to build the matchmaking business, not give it a black eye," he said. "Doing what she was asking felt a lot like crossing an ethical line."

"Yeah. And she also lied to me by not being where she said she was going to be. Someday she'll understand. I need to know that she's safe. It's unacceptable to exploit my faith in her, and she has to pay a price. Losing a little freedom seems like the appropriate way to get my point across."

Gabe studied her face, the lines of tension that pulled her full lips tight. "Something tells me it's harder on you than her."

"It isn't easy being the enforcer," she admitted. "I have to work, so she's on her honor to take the bus straight home from school and stay there unless prior arrangements have been made. Like the day she went rogue. She was supposed to go home with a friend and didn't. I don't want to confiscate her phone, because then I can't contact her." She sighed. "And when I'm at home with her, she's a sulky and mouthy kid pushing back against what she sees as unfair and unjust punishment. I have to make this a painful lesson, but doesn't it seem wrong that it hurts me the most? That I'm the one who's miserable?"

Just then Toni brought a tray with their coffee and Courtney's scone. After setting everything on the table, she said, "Is there anything else I can get you? Cream for your coffee?"

"Black is fine," he told her, then looked at the woman across from him. "You?"

Courtney shook her head. "This is good for me."

"We're fine," Gabe told the teen.

"Okay. If you need refills or anything, let me know. Enjoy."

"Thanks."

When the server walked away, Gabe watched Courtney dig into her scone. Something told him she hadn't eaten any of the goodwill pizza she'd brought home. "So tell me about those negotiations I saved you from."

She chewed a bite, then washed it down with latte. "Except for her resentment and unhappiness, everything about her being grounded works for me."

"How?"

"Her room is neat as a pin. According to her, she has no social life." She smiled. "Putting on hold the boy/girl stuff even for two weeks is a plus as far as I'm concerned. But she's complaining that I'm destroying her social life. It's the end of the world, in her opinion, because I'm too strict."

"Sounds like high drama."

"You have no idea." She rolled her eyes. "And somehow she connected her nonexistent social life with my pathetic one. One minute I was explaining the advantages of telling the truth. The next, she promised that if I went on one date, she'd stop badgering me for a whole month."

He grinned. "If she ever does become a lawyer, I'd put her on retainer in a heartbeat."

"I know, right?" She smiled, then turned serious. "Her other terms were that if I got a boyfriend, she'd leave me alone for a whole year."

That gave him the perfect segue. "I feel your pain."

"I know you don't have a teen on restriction who's trying to convince you dating is a good thing," she said wryly.

"True." And that was his fault. "But my mom and aunt and the rest of my family are engaged in a conspiracy to drive me crazy."

"I don't think it's possible that they're worse than Ava."

"Prepare to be convinced." He held his lukewarm cup between his hands. "They invited Ember to Sunday dinner."

"I'm sorry. Ember? That's a person?"

"Her name is Ember Kiley, and she's a very attractive woman who is trying to break into modeling. My mother works in a dermatology office, and

Ember is a patient. Trying to perfect her already flawless skin."

"I see."

"I'm not finished yet." He sipped his coffee, then swallowed his annoyance along with the bitter liquid. "Sunday dinner is a family tradition. Don't get me wrong—it's one I like. Except the part where a different age-appropriate woman is invited every week and ends up sitting beside me."

"They're not subtle, are they? Your family." Courtney's voice was sympathetic.

"Not even close. I decided to say something. Ask them to cease and desist. No, I begged them, actually."

"Since you called me to commiserate, I'm guessing it didn't go well."

"That's an understatement." He looked at her. "Have you ever seen the look of disappointment a mom gets on her face? The one where you're not meeting her expectations."

"Yeah. And I'll never forget it." Amusement disappeared, and her expression was full of memories that didn't look pleasant. "It was disappointment times a hundred when I told her I was pregnant. Not long after, I had nowhere to live."

Gabe's question had been glib, facetious. He remembered her telling him this and regretted bringing up what must have been an incredibly traumatic event in her life. "Courtney, I'm sorry. You told me about it in the office that day. That was really thoughtless of me."

She waved away his apology. "No problem. I wasn't going for the sympathy vote. It was a long time ago. So far my disappointed-mom look hasn't yielded results, but I keep it around for emergencies. Just wanted to let you know I understand where you're coming from."

"I guess you do." He let out a long breath. Throwing women at him wasn't even in the same league with kicking out a pregnant teenager. And look at her now. His respect and admiration for her doubled. "I know I have no right to complain about my loving but interfering family."

"Of course you do," she protested. "I get it. Ava loves me, too, but the meddling isn't any easier to take from a child or any other relative. So what did they do when you asked them to stop?"

"They played the wrong card. As in they're concerned about me, and worry causes stress that can take years off your life."

"Guilt." She nodded knowingly. "I know it well. I'm ruining my daughter's social life because I grounded her for going to a matchmaker to find me a man. It's so embarrassing."

"Tell me about it." There was so much kindness, compassion and understanding in her big brown eyes that he wanted to sink right into them. For several moments, he was quiet, then felt the urge to fill that silence with words. Any words he could think of. "They actually said that I need to get back in the saddle."

"And how do you feel about that?"

"I don't even want to see a saddle."

Half of her scone was still on her plate, apparently forgotten after his confession. She met his gaze, and her own was serious. "You said on the phone that you might have a fix for the problem. Care to share?"

When Gabe had made the call, he hadn't been completely sure about this idea. Still, he'd figured reaching out couldn't hurt. In business he'd learned to go with his gut, and talking to Courtney would convince him one way or the other. They both understood family interference, and that conversation had led him to this crossroad. But he'd made up his mind when she walked into the coffee shop and unleashed those killer dimples when she smiled.

"I have a proposition for you," he started.

"Oh?" Her expression turned wary.

"You're probably going to think this is crazy. The most out-there thing you ever heard."

"Should I be afraid?" she asked.

"You tell me." *Here goes*, he thought. "I think we should fake date."

Chapter Four

When Gabe said "fake date," Courtney was just swallowing a sip of coffee. She nearly spit it out. Then she started coughing and hoped nothing was coming out of her nose.

"Are you okay?" Gabe started to slide out of the booth and looked as if he was going to do the Heimlich maneuver on her.

"I'm fine," she managed to say. He signaled Toni for a glass of water, and she took a drink. "Sorry. I thought I heard you say we should fake date."

"I did."

A couple seconds passed while she waited for him to crack a smile and say, "Gotcha." He didn't. If anything, he looked more intense and brooding than when he'd told her about Ember and the family dinner.

"You're kidding, right?" She had to make sure she wasn't being punked.

"I'm completely serious," he confirmed.

"You're right."

"I am?"

She nodded. "This is the craziest thing I've ever heard."

"No. Of course," he said. "Figured I'd just throw it out there. After Ember... No big deal— You're probably right."

"Not so fast." She held up a hand to stop his words. "It's out there now. That doesn't mean I'm not curious. Very, very curious."

"Okay."

"I have many questions," she said.

"Shoot."

Courtney couldn't believe she was actually discussing this as if it was a serious consideration. It couldn't hurt to at least understand what he was talking about. "What does fake dating mean?"

"It's like dating but not real. We go out, pretend to be interested in each other and get my family to stop inviting strange women over for dinner. And your daughter will cease and desist nagging you about having a boyfriend."

Courtney was somewhat distracted by his boyish good looks and the touch of sheepishness in his expression. Then his words sank in. "So, in essence, we would be lying to the people we love."

"Wrong thing," he admitted. "But I submit that it's for the right reason. We'd be eliminating stress and worry, possibly prolonging their lives."

"That's a stretch. And still a lie." She was trying to wrap her head around the craziest thing she'd ever heard.

"Look at it this way." He thought for a moment. "We'll just go out. Friends having a good time. Getting to know each other. People do that all the time."

"But what would we do?"

"Good question. It's been a while since I dated."

"Me, too." She broke off a piece of the scone on her plate and nervously crushed it between her thumb and index finger.

"What do you like to do?" he asked.

That question gave her pause. "Everything revolves around what my daughter wants to do. I haven't really thought about what I want for a long time."

"What do you and Ava do?"

"Shop. Lunch. Movies." She shrugged. "But she's spending more and more time with her friends. I've noticed lately that being seen with her mom is getting embarrassing. She doesn't try very hard to hide it."

His look was sympathetic. "That's normal."

"I know." She was getting sad about her little girl growing up. It was time to turn the question back on him. "What do you like to do?"

"Shopping is not on my recreational activities list. And I can't remember the last movie I saw. Mostly I work."

"And I thought I was pathetic."

He laughed. "Apparently that award goes to me."

"Maybe our loved ones have a point." Courtney wondered if Ava was mature beyond her years and could see that her mother's life was out of balance. "Maybe we do need other interests besides work and child rearing."

His eyebrows pulled together as he thought that over. "Even if they're right, the approach is overkill. I don't know about you, but my response to pressure isn't positive. It brings out my stubborn streak."

"Me, too."

The idea of "seeing" Gabe didn't suck, she realized. And if it got Ava off her back, she could figure out her own social life without the burden of pleasing her daughter. Or disappointing her. Gabe had mentioned worry and life expectancy in terms of his parents, but kids could guilt you just as much. Maybe more.

"You've been quiet over there awhile." Gabe toyed with the half-empty coffee mug on the table in front of him. "What are you thinking? Probably that I should have my head examined."

"Actually, maybe I need a psych eval, too," she admitted. "Your idea is intriguing and might possibly have merit. It's gone from the craziest thing I ever heard to don't be so quick to blow it off."

"Oh?" His blue eyes gleamed with interest.

"How long do you think we'd have to 'go out'?" She put air quotes around the last two words.

"That's flexible, I think." He relaxed in the booth

and stretched his arm out along the top. "We'll take it one 'date' at a time." Now he was using air quotes. "We can gather data and evaluate. When it feels right, we'll break things off. Afterward we'll be sad for an appropriate length of time. The whole process could take as little or as long as we see fit. But keep in mind that for the duration of the process, the meddlers will leave us in peace."

"It sounds like heaven. And yet—underhanded." She met his gaze. "You make it sound so very easy to be underhanded. Should I be worried?"

"I can provide references if you want," he teased. "My aunt Lil would vouch for me in glowing terms."

"What about your mom?"

"She's prejudiced. In my favor." He lifted one shoulder in a shrug. "It's a mom thing."

"You're right. Moms think their kids are perfect." At least Courtney thought Ava was. "In spite of their flaws."

"Yeah."

"So we should talk about ground rules," she suggested. "Just in case we really decide to do this."

"Okay." He looked at her. "You start. What do you think is most important?"

"Hmm."

She thought about past relationships—not that this would be one. But she'd stayed in her marriage too long after realizing the man she married was a selfish ass. He'd promised he wanted to be a father to Ava, but the ink was barely dry on the marriage certificate before he was talking about having "real" kids. She should have left right then, but she'd tried to make the mistake work. Never again. That was three years ago, and she hadn't dated since.

"Here's one," she said. "Either of us can end it at any time. For any reason."

"Or no reason." He nodded. "Agreed."

"Do you have anything?"

"It should be fun," he said thoughtfully. "I enjoy spending time with you."

"Really? Even when I'm dumping my whole life story on you?" She could almost laugh about that day in his office. At this moment she was slightly less mortified.

"You were upset and had low blood sugar. It happens." He shrugged. "But fun is good. When that stops, we 'break up.'"

"Sensible." Courtney realized that she told Ava everything. She always tried to be up front, honest and straightforward with her daughter. And even Courtney's girlfriends talked to Ava. That would blow the lid off this. "I just thought of something. Probably we don't need to spell it out, but—"

"What?"

"Only the two of us can know. The only way a secret stays secret is if you don't tell anyone."

"Very clandestine." He grinned.

Holy moly! When he smiled, her worldview tilted just a little. She felt the power of that look all the way to her toes. If they stuck to the "having fun" rule, it could happen a lot. She hoped that wouldn't be a problem.

"I guess it's a thing with me because of my job." She shrugged. "Patient privacy is a very big deal."

"Makes sense."

They looked at each other for several moments without saying anything as she tried to come up with more ground rules and couldn't. "Surely there's more that we should define about this."

"I know, right? Seems too easy, too good to be true." He looked out the window for a moment. "The thing is, you seem like an incredibly reasonable woman."

"I am. And you appear to be an amazingly reasonable man."

"So what about this? If anything comes up, we'll discuss it like the two reasonable adults we are and adjust the ground rules as necessary?"

"That sounds incredibly—reasonable." She smiled.

He blew out a breath. "In that case… Are we going to do this?"

Courtney thought about her options. If she turned down this opportunity, she would risk Ava possibly doing something more drastic to fix her up. Something that didn't include an honest and trustworthy Gabe. Plus, the nagging would continue. Did that make her officially desperate? Yeah, it kinda did. And yet…

"It does seem too easy," she said. "Shouldn't it be more complicated?"

"I suppose I can complicate the heck out of it if you want me to," he teased.

She laughed. "No. My life is already complex."

"If you have any doubt, we'll just forget I ever suggested it. Not a problem."

And that sensible, rational, logical response was what positively made up her mind. She put out her hand to shake on the deal. "We are doing this."

Gabe reached out and said, "To a mutually beneficial arrangement. It's like an insurance policy on the risks and hazards of relationships."

His words made perfect sense. Right up until he touched her. He curved his big hand around hers, and tingles danced up her arm. It was suddenly hard to breathe, let alone think rationally.

"To a non-relationship." She pulled her hand away and tried to smile.

If she'd touched him first, would she have gone through with this deal? Maybe. But it might have taken her longer to agree, or she might have asked for a cooling-off period. She'd made a lot of mistakes where men were concerned, and she fervently hoped that she hadn't just done it again. Still, she'd negotiated walking away at any time for any reason. How bad could it be? What harm could giving this a whirl do?

Ava plopped down on Courtney's bed to review her first-date-with-Gabriel outfit. She looked her up and down, then said, "You're welcome."

"For what?" Glancing in her freestanding full-length mirror, Courtney critically assessed her black slacks and silky white blouse with ruffles at the sleeves and neck.

"If I hadn't gone to Make Me a Match, you wouldn't be going out with Mr. Blackburne tonight." Rolling onto her tummy, she cupped her cheeks in her palms. "Come to think of it, I should be ungrounded. What I did was a public service."

"How do you figure?"

"If I hadn't made that bold move, the two of you would never have met. He wouldn't have called you for a date and you'd be spending another boring night at home by yourself."

It wasn't a complete lie that Gabe had called her. Courtney just left out the part where the "date" wasn't real. "But I wouldn't be alone. Because you're still grounded."

She was going out, but the evening could still be boring. At least the scenery would be fun to look at. Gabriel Blackburne was a very nice-looking man. She enjoyed talking to him, and hopefully he hadn't already used up his good material.

"Mom, you're so unreasonable. I'm going to appeal my sentence to the Supreme Court."

"By the time they heard your argument, you'd be old enough to unground yourself."

"It's so unfair," Ava grumbled. "And that blouse makes you look like you've been swallowed by the ruffle monster."

"You're right." Courtney sighed, then pulled it off and tossed it on the bed with the other two she'd decided against. "I knew it didn't look right, but I don't know what to wear. Everything in my closet is old and wrong."

"Where is he taking you?"

"Out to dinner."

"But *where*? Fast food or candles and white tablecloths?"

"I don't know."

Courtney couldn't tell Ava that she might have missed key details because Gabe's deep, husky phone voice had caused an electrical short in her brain. She'd taken the call in front of Ava and had to make sure her responses were convincing. That had been a lot of pressure, and some of the information had been lost in the process. Clearly she should have taken drama classes instead of going into the nursing program.

"Okay," Ava said thoughtfully. "I can work with that."

She rolled off the floral-patterned comforter and marched into Courtney's walk-in closet. Moments later she came out with tailored dark jeans, a classy white T-shirt, a navy blazer and three-inch wedge sandals. "This outfit will go almost anywhere, Mom."

Courtney blinked at the clothes her daughter set on the bed. "It's perfect. When did you get so fashionably brilliant?"

"I can't believe you haven't noticed." Ava gave her a "duh" look. "But what else should I expect?

I'm dealing with the woman who grounded me for no good reason."

"I'll admit that I'm distracted," she said, "but not *that* distracted. I had a very good reason. Someday you'll thank me for teaching you the difference between right and wrong."

"So it was wrong to want you to be happy?"

"No. That part was incredibly sweet. It's the being untruthful about where you were that's a problem." Courtney pulled off the black slacks and replaced them with the jeans and T-shirt. "In or out?"

"Tuck it. Show off your tiny waist," Ava suggested.

"Do I need a belt? Do I *have* a belt?"

"Seriously? I can't believe I have to do everything." The teen disappeared into the closet again and came out holding a simple navy belt with silver accents. "This is perfect."

When that was in place, Courtney slipped on the blazer and checked herself out in the mirror. But after the ruffle debacle, her judgment was damaged. "How do I look? Do I look stupid? Maybe I'm trying too hard. What's the verdict?"

"You look amazing, Mom, except…"

"What?" She turned to examine herself from the back. "Is there a spot somewhere? Did I back up into paint without realizing it? Do these pants make my butt look like an oil tanker?"

"No. It's your makeup."

"What about it?"

Ava studied her critically. "I'm thinking more drama. Maybe a smoky eye. Definitely there should be more intensity."

As far as Courtney was concerned, fake dating was already dramatic and intense enough. Her stomach was churning even though clothes and makeup didn't matter. Tonight was a sham. A charade. A con. She'd admit, though, that clothes were kind of important. Avoiding public nakedness was a good goal. Plus she didn't want to be embarrassed. In fact, there was a part of her that wanted to prove to Gabe that she could attract a man, in spite of what her daughter's desperation probably made him think.

But she wasn't looking to impress him for the long term, because nothing was going to come of this. There wouldn't be a future. Except she had to convince Ava that she was sincerely trying to look her best. That made her feel like a fraud, probably because that's exactly what she was. And, for the record, this was harder than she'd expected when discussing it at Coffee Break.

"This makeup is perfectly fine. It's what I wear to work," Courtney protested.

"Rookie dating mistake." Ava pointed to the antique dressing table and bench on the far bedroom wall. "Sit."

Courtney wondered if that's how she looked when issuing commands to her daughter, then meekly did as she was told. It was a question for another time.

Her cosmetics were neatly arranged, and Ava looked through everything, gauging what she had to work with. She chose a coral blush and applied it to Courtney's cheeks, then blended so the effect gave her color, but subtly. Then she picked out shades of shadows that made her chocolate-brown eyes look huge and, dare she say it, smoky. Darkening her brows and thickening her lashes with mascara came last.

"Wow, sweetie. I don't look like myself."

"It's you, but better," Ava assured her. "Now the final touch. Lipstick."

"Please, no red."

"Ew." Ava wrinkled her nose as she looked through the limited choices. "I was thinking something neutral, leaning toward warm and earthy undertones. Oh. This is perfect. Girls' night out."

"So this is life imitating makeup? Or makeup imitating life?"

"Don't complicate it, Mom." She dabbed on the creamy color and said again, "You're welcome."

Courtney looked at herself in the mirror. The effect was most definitely dramatic and intense. So now her outside matched the feelings on the inside. In a good way. "How did you learn to do this?"

"My friends and I fool around with makeup and stuff when we get together." Ava shrugged and added, "But I've been in solitary for so long, there's probably all kinds of techniques I don't know about. And my friends have probably moved on without me. I probably don't have any friends."

"You don't have much longer to go." Courtney smiled at her child's tragic expression. "And just think of how much you have to look forward to when the restriction is lifted."

"No one will even remember me," Ava complained. "I'll be an outcast."

"Then they weren't really your friends in the first place."

"Silly me." Ava sighed and rolled her eyes. "I didn't think you would understand."

Courtney understood completely, and in a way she never wanted Ava to. Getting pregnant and having a baby had cut her off completely from the high school life she'd taken for granted and the kids she'd thought would always be there. And she hadn't really had the luxury of grieving over the loss. She'd been too frightened about keeping a roof over her head and food to feed herself and the baby growing inside her. She was actually glad that Ava thought being grounded was the worst thing in the world. That meant she didn't face the basics of survival.

"Sweetie, thank you for your help. Now I need to see this outfit with the shoes." She slipped them on and stood. She was used to walking around in sneakers for a twelve-hour shift at the hospital. Wearing these wedges for twelve minutes might be a challenge. "Wow, what in the world made me buy these shoes? They're the exact opposite of comfortable."

"But they look great. And he's pretty tall, Mom. You'll look weird next to him without the extra height." Ava seemed pleased with the results of her efforts. "Mom, you're really hot. I guarantee Mr. Blackburne will think so, too."

No, he wouldn't, she thought. He was just using her for cover from his family. And Courtney was using him right back to keep Ava in line. Still, the guilt was crushing her, and she almost blurted out the truth. Nerves were like that. When they were jumping inside you like drops of water on a hot skillet, it loosened a person's tongue.

Courtney was just about to spill her guts when the doorbell sounded. She looked at the bedside clock. "Oh God, he's here. And he's early."

"That's a good sign that he's perfect for you, the woman whose motto is 'if you're not five minutes early, you're already late.'" Ava headed out of the room. "I'll go answer the door. Take your time. Don't look too eager. Be cool. Aloof."

Before Courtney could ask where she was getting her dating advice, the teen was gone. Was she too eager? She'd had a good time with him at Coffee Break, planning this scheme. He was smart, funny and, as she'd thought before, not hard on the eyes. Apparently he didn't hold the meltdown in his office against her. Points to him. Her daughter had pronounced him a nice man. But men didn't always live up to their advanced billing. Sometimes they were just out for what they could get, and they would use anyone necessary to do that. But she and Gabe had taken care of that ahead of time, so this should meet both their needs.

Thank goodness she and Gabe were on the same page, with the same agenda. And an insurance pol-

icy. She could end this at any time without an explanation. And so could he.

Courtney looked in the mirror one last time and
blew out a breath. "You got this."

She left the sanctuary of her room and walked
down the stairs. Voices drifted to her. One deep and
unbearably sexy. The other impossibly young and
excited. *Here we go*, she thought. *Showtime.*

Gabe was in the living room chatting with Ava
when Courtney walked in. Whatever he was saying
seemed to be forgotten as he stopped midsentence
and stared at her.

"Hi, Gabe," she said.

"Courtney. Hi." He smiled. "You look beautiful."

"Thanks." She suddenly realized that this was
the first time he'd seen her in something other than
shapeless scrubs. And she'd been worried about
being appropriately dressed. This was a step up. On
top of that, he was channeling a similar vibe—jeans,
a shirt with button-down collar and a tweed sports
coat. Loafers completed his look and were probably
more comfortable than her wedges.

Then Courtney looked up at him and was glad
Ava had insisted on shoes that added a couple inches
to her height. He *was* very tall.

"Where are you taking her?" Ava asked.

"Patrick's Pub." A dark look flashed through his
eyes and hinted at a story behind the choice of their
first "date."

She made a mental note to ask him about it later. "I haven't been there since it was remodeled."

"My older brother was married there."

"Oh?"

"It was a pretty nontraditional wedding. The bride wore red."

"Cool," Ava said.

"It was. The atmosphere is casual and fun, something for everyone. And the food is great," he said.

"Text me a picture, Mom."

"We'll get a selfie," Gabe promised. "Are you still grounded?"

"Yes." She groaned, then a sly expression replaced her tragic look. "Don't you think it's unfair?"

"Nice try, kid." He grinned and held up his hands in a gesture of surrender. "No way I'm touching that on a first date."

"But I need someone on my side," Ava protested.

"I sympathize, but I have to be Switzerland on this."

Ava frowned at him. "What does that mean?"

"I'm neutral."

"You're just trying to impress my mom."

He looked at Courtney. "Your daughter is very smart and perceptive. Just like her mother."

This man would turn female heads everywhere he went. And he was very smooth. If he was nervous about what they were doing, it didn't show. He was nothing but cool and confident, and she couldn't help wondering if he'd done this before. After all, fake dating had been his idea.

The day they met, she'd wished she could hear his talk to the high school kids, see if he was as interesting as he seemed. She was about to find out.

He looked at her. "You ready to go?"

"Yes."

This felt a lot like jumping into the deep end of the pool.

Chapter Five

"I haven't been that nervous since meeting my wife's father for the first time." Gabe glanced over at Courtney in the front passenger seat of his sporty Mercedes, then back at the road.

"Really? That was just my daughter. And you don't strike me as the nervous type."

"I'm not. That's why it's noteworthy."

"But this isn't even the first time you met Ava." She paused for a moment then added, "It's actually the third time."

"True. But the other times, I wasn't picking up her mother to take her out on a date." He gently braked the car to a stop at a red light. "In fact, I've never taken anyone's mother out on a date. That puts a lot of pressure on a guy. Take my word for it."

"I think it's probably because this isn't real. The tension you felt was most likely guilt." She nodded sagely. "I was feeling it, too, getting ready."

"In what way?"

She hesitated as if choosing her words carefully. "I felt as if I was playing a part. Putting on an act about what to wear and how I looked when it really doesn't matter. We both know what's going to happen. It's like reading the end of a book first. And because of that, she's the one I'm trying to impress, not you."

And yet she had. Courtney Davidson was a very beautiful woman. He was a guy. He noticed. It didn't have to mean anything.

"True," he said. "Was Ava happy you're going out?"

"She was excited when you called and asked me to dinner. In fact, she is claiming all the credit. She declared in no uncertain terms that if she hadn't gone to Make Me a Match, it would never have happened. And she says I should take her off restriction for performing a public service."

"But you stuck to your guns."

"Can't show weakness." There was a smile in her voice when she said, "After she finished protesting my negative response, she did my eye makeup."

"She's a great kid."

"You'll get no argument from me."

"And we're here." He turned left into the strip mall parking lot where Patrick's Pub was located. It was Friday night, and there were lots of cars. "Looks like a popular place."

"Yeah."

"Carla, my aunt's assistant, is friends with the owner. Tess and her now husband became partners when he invested capital to give this place a facelift to improve business."

"Looks like it worked."

"Yeah. Carla met her fiancé here on ladies' night." He opened his door, and the overhead light flashed on, revealing her surprise.

"Oh? Should I be worried?"

"No. I didn't pick it with a romantic agenda in mind. My purpose is much more practical than that."

When he came around and opened her door, she asked, "Care to enlighten me?"

"I'm doing business research."

"Nice work if you can get it," she said wryly.

"Let me provide context." He thought for a moment as she slid out of the car. They fell into step, walking toward the pub. "My aunt is a bighearted romantic who wants everyone to find love. One of the Make Me a Match promotions is a first date, and she thinks the agency should pull out all the stops. Atmosphere, muted lighting, fresh flowers, French food and candles."

"Sounds expensive."

"It is. Aunt Lil and I had a discussion about it, and she was unwilling to compromise. That's when Carla mentioned that this is where she met her husband-to-be."

Courtney stepped up on the sidewalk and nodded her approval. "So you're checking it out. Multi-tasking."

His hand was on the door, ready to open it for her when she smiled at him and unleashed her dimples. It was astonishing how fast a man with an above-average IQ could go from articulate to speechless simply because of a woman's smile.

"So," she said, "let's go multitask. I'm happy to provide the female point of view for your work research."

"Right." He grabbed the handle and pulled the solid door open. "After you."

They walked inside and looked around. The interior hadn't changed since his brother's wedding, except the crowd was all strangers instead of family. It was actually a relief not to know anyone. He didn't have to keep up pretenses in front of the people who knew him best.

A long bar was straight ahead, and booths lined the perimeter of the room. There was live music, and couples were dancing in the area set off for it. To the left was a separate room with pool tables and a flat-screen TV to televise sporting events. A baseball game was on now. Next to it was a restaurant with booths and tables.

Gabe pointed it out. "I think that's what we're looking for over there."

"Works for me," she shouted over the music.

He settled his hand at the small of her back, an automatic, intimate gesture that still felt rusty, clumsy.

Something he hadn't done in a long time. Something he'd missed doing.

"There's a corner booth," he said. "It's quiet in here."

She nodded and headed for it, then slid onto the bench seat. Looking around, she said, "This part is new."

He nodded. The lights were dim, but no flowers or white tablecloths decorated the table. No candles, either. But cozy pictures of taverns and lighthouses hung on the walls. It seemed like a good place to talk and get to know someone. That was Make Me a Match information he tucked away. Because suddenly Courtney was quiet. She was doing her own inspection of the decor, looking everywhere and at anything but him.

The silence stretched between them. It was odd, because every other time he'd seen her, they'd had no trouble finding something to say. Even in the car on the way here, conversation had flowed freely. But that was in the dark. Now that they were actually "on a date," the awkwardness was like an unwanted chaperone.

They did know how this was going to go. Courtney was right about that. But one of their rules was to have fun. Go through the motions of getting to know each other. That required communication, and he had a plan.

A server walked over to their table. "I'm Marie, and I'll be taking care of you tonight. Can I get you something to drink?"

"I'd like a glass of chardonnay," Courtney said.

"Beer for me."

"Coming right up." She put menus in front of them. "You can look these over while you're waiting. Unless you're ready to order now."

Courtney opened one. "There's a lot here. You've been here before, Gabe. What do you like?"

"Wow. Everything." He thought for a moment. "But if you make me choose, I'd have to say the seafood risotto or trout amandine."

"I need a minute." Courtney looked at the server, then across the table at him. "Unless you're ready."

"No." He hadn't even opened the menu, because he was too caught up in trying to figure out what she was thinking.

"Take your time," Marie said. "I'll get those drinks then check on you in a bit."

"Thanks." He glanced at Courtney, but she was still focused on checking out the food choices and holding that menu up like a shield.

Gabe reached into his inside jacket pocket and pulled out several folded pieces of paper. He figured it best to confront this head-on. "Do you feel as awkward as I do?"

Her gaze lifted to his. "Yes. And it's weird, because I didn't expect this."

"My aunt did."

"Wait—what?" She blinked at him. "She knows about this?"

"Not our arrangement, if that's what you're asking. Just that I was taking you out to dinner. It's important to get the word out to my family, and Aunt Lil is the best way to do that." He thought about it and felt a little bit bad about deceiving his family. But what they didn't know wouldn't hurt them, and they'd never find out. "My guess is that everyone already has the four-one-one on us by now."

"Okay."

"She was delighted, by the way. In case you were wondering."

"No, I—" She stopped and shook her head. "Of course I was wondering. So she approved of you asking out the woman whose daughter goes rogue in your office?"

"She thought you and Ava are both charming. And actually said she wished she'd thought of pairing us up at Sunday dinner."

"Ember would be heartbroken."

"She'll survive," he said wryly.

She grinned, then pointed to the papers he was holding. "What do you have there?"

"Dating profiles." He handed several sheets across the table to her. "The one Ava filled out for you and the other one I did for me."

"Really? I thought you were going to destroy mine."

"Yeah." He'd put it on his desk but never got around to shredding it. Why was that? "I've been busy. It slipped my mind."

Courtney seemed to accept that, but it could have been she was preoccupied checking out the first page of what he'd given her. She started to hand it back. "This is yours. You must have mixed them up."

"No. You read mine. I'll pick random questions, and we'll see what Ava said. According to Aunt Lil, this will be helpful in getting to know each other."

"It could get more awkward," she warned. But there was laughter in her eyes. "I have no idea what Ava might have said pretending to be me."

"And that's the cool part. It doesn't matter because we aren't about impressing each other. This is just for fun."

"True." She tucked a strand of silky brown hair behind her ear. "Shall I start?"

"Ladies first."

"Ahem." She skimmed his first page, then cleared her throat. "'What two or three things do you enjoy doing in your free time?' Your answer—work, work and more work. Seriously, Gabe?"

"At Make Me a Match, we advise clients to be brutally honest on these things. The fact is, I like to work."

"You left part two of the question blank. What you do on a typical day off."

He'd gotten in the habit of not having leisure time. It provided too much opportunity to dwell on things. "Days off are rare. I reserve them for obligatory family stuff."

"A workaholic." She shrugged. "I should have known when you combined our fake date with a work thing."

"I thought you said I was multitasking."

"Now I know better," she said. "That profile you filled out puts a finer point on it."

He hadn't always been this way. "Let's see what your daughter said about you."

"Oh boy."

He scanned the paper. "So, your leisure time is spent going to movies, reading books and hanging out with your daughter."

"She's got quite the imagination. Those are the things I like to do. But reality is more like cleaning house, shopping for groceries and nagging said daughter to clean her room and do her homework."

He laughed. "So, you're a workaholic, too."

"By necessity, not choice. Like you." Her look said she wondered why that was.

For him it had happened because of fate. Margo died. It was out of his control, and he had a hard time reconciling that. Their server delivered their drinks and said she'd be back in a few minutes to take their orders.

"Okay," he said. "Let's do another one. I'll go first this time."

"Be my guest."

"'What are you passionate about?'" he read.

"I can hardly wait to hear Ava's response." She took a sip of ice-cold wine, then waited.

He looked at the page and read, "'I'm passionate about being a nurse, saving lives, getting patients back on their feet and helping them live their healthiest lives.'"

"Wow. That's actually true. I didn't realize Ava

knew me that well. She was listening." Courtney looked surprised and pleased. She held up the paper. "Now you."

"Remember I did this in a hurry."

"Disclaimer noted," she teased. Then she read, "'I'm passionate about career and family.' That was short and sweet."

"Those two things speak for themselves."

"Family, maybe. But what makes you passionate about your work? Off the top of your head. Elaborate."

He thought for a moment. "I like saving companies from ruin."

"You're a knight in shining armor. A rescuer."

"Nothing so romantic. I don't like failure or waste. Preventing both energizes me."

"Hmm. That's still noble," she said.

"Takes one to know one. You save lives."

"Just doing my job," she insisted humbly.

He'd been glancing through the questionnaire, and one of Ava's answers made him laugh. "This one is, 'Would you date someone who has children?'"

"Oh my gosh. What did she say?"

"I quote—'I can't even believe there's any question about that. Anyone who wouldn't go out with someone who has kids is just a jerk to be avoided. Children are awesome.'"

She groaned. "Ava might as well have said her mom is just desperate to find a man."

"But we both know that's not true," he said. "We are here because her mother *doesn't* want a man."

"Impressive. You are a man who listens. Now let's see how you answered that one." She ran her index finger down the page to find what she was looking for. When she did, her eyebrows rose. "You say right here that you like children."

"Why are you surprised?"

"I guess I shouldn't be. You don't have any kids, yet you filled in at the last minute for a freshman motivational talk at the high school, and you tutor math. Finally, you didn't throw Ava out of your office. Actions speak louder than words."

He shrugged. "Just the truth and nothing but."

"Ava's right. Even though until tonight you've never taken anyone's mother out on a date, you're a nice man, Gabriel Blackburne."

"It's our secret." He liked the way she was looking at him, as if he'd done something wonderful. But he hadn't. "Are you ready to order yet?"

"Yes. I'm starving."

"Okay, then." He signaled their server.

Gabe found that he was hungry, too, and not just for food. But he would deal with that later. For now the ice was broken and the awkwardness disappeared. They ordered dinner and split a decadent triple chocolate dessert after solemnly promising not to feel guilty about it. Conversation flowed nonstop about everything from raising Ava to sports and books. Time seemed to stand still. As much as he unexpectedly found himself wishing that was the case, it didn't.

"Holy cow," Courtney said after looking at her

watch. She appeared to be genuinely disappointed. "It's getting late, and I have to work tomorrow. We should probably—"

"Yeah. I'll take you home."

"And we've monopolized this table. I'm feeling bad for Marie. We've cost her money in tips."

"Not to worry. She received a very generous one. That made her happy, along with the fact that her shift was just a little easier because we took up one of her tables."

"You paid the check?" When he nodded, she asked, "When?"

"You were in the ladies' room."

"But I was going to split it with you," she protested. "It's only fair since this isn't really a date. We're both getting something out of this, and my investment should be the same as yours."

"It's no big deal."

She pulled out her wallet and started to remove some bills. "I'll give you my share now."

"I can't let a woman pay for dinner. It might make me a chauvinist, but I can live with that. My parents didn't raise me to let a woman split the check when I asked her out."

"That's incredibly sweet and annoying at the same time." She sighed. "I'll pick up the next one."

No way he would let her, but that was a discussion for another time. "We'll deal with that when it comes up."

"You're already not going to let me, right?" Her

eyes narrowed on him. "This is a rule we should have discussed."

"Which is why we agreed that if anything comes up, we can adjust the ground rules accordingly."

"Okay." She put away her wallet and picked up her purse. "From now on, if there's a check involved, we will split it. Consider the rules adjusted."

Over his dead body. "You're very bossy."

She grinned. "Oh, and thank you for dinner."

"You're welcome."

Gabe drove back to her place and walked her to the door. The condo porch light was on, and Courtney fitted her key into the lock.

She looked up at him and smiled. "That went well, I think. We can evaluate the results with our families and compare notes on the reaction."

"Okay." He would agree to anything if she kept smiling at him like that. "You look pleased about something."

"Yes. I just had a thought."

"Are you going to just keep grinning? Or do you plan to tell me?"

She glanced around to make sure she wasn't overheard. "We don't have to muddle through the first-date good-night-kiss pressure. That's such a relief."

"Yeah."

That was a flat-out lie. She'd leaned toward him to whisper this observation, and her breath skimmed his cheek. The scent of her skin crept inside him and touched off fires everywhere. His body was feeling the heat. Dating might be a pretense, but wanting to kiss her was all too real. All night the prospect of doing it had popped into his mind every time he looked at her mouth.

This was something else that hadn't surfaced in their conversation about setting parameters. He was trying to come up with a fix to the problem when the door suddenly opened. Light from inside spilled over them, and Ava stood there.

"I heard voices out here." She looked at her mother. "Just invite him in, Mom. I'm still up and bored, what with being grounded while you went out and had fun."

Courtney's eyes widened when she looked at him. "It's up to Gabe. Would you like to come in?"

Choices, he thought. His lonely rented condo all by himself, or lively conversation with Courtney and Ava. But, once again, that wasn't in the ground rules.

"It's getting late. Your mom has to work tomorrow. So, I'll say good-night." He leaned forward and kissed Courtney's cheek, a quick, impersonal touch. All it did was make him want more. "I'll call you."

"Okay. Good night, Gabe. And thanks again for dinner."

He walked back to his car, feeling a little unsettled. Probably because he hadn't let himself feel anything for a long time. There was no denying his attraction to Courtney, and he hadn't factored that into the fake-date equation. Thank goodness for Ava. The interruption had stopped him. If he'd kissed Courtney, she'd think he was one more jerk taking advantage of a situation that wasn't real.

He hadn't expected this strong reaction and realized he should have. She was a beautiful woman, and he was a guy responding to her. Things weren't any more complicated than that. So, problem solved.

After changing into her pajamas, Courtney was in the bathroom taking off the pound of makeup on her face. A little wistfully she dragged the washcloth over her cheek, the spot where Gabriel had kissed her. It was impersonal, just for show, when Ava had interrupted them. If Courtney had turned her head at just the right moment, his lips would have found hers. And what would that have been like?

The thought made her shiver in an unfamiliar yet delicious way. But indulging the fantasy of this being more than they'd agreed to was asking for trouble. That peck on the cheek was nothing more than a charade, and she needed to remember that.

"Knock, knock." Ava walked into the bathroom and sat on the side of the tub. "How did it go?"

Courtney wanted to say it had gone better than planned but bit back the words. That would require an explanation and make the whole pretense blow up. "Dinner?"

She realized soap and water wasn't working on the eye makeup and wet a cotton swab with mascara remover. "The food was great. I had seafood risotto. Would have brought you leftovers, but we finished everything. Gabe had trout amandine and gave me a bite. Really good, too. And then we shared a dessert. Chocolate. Finished that, too—"

"Mom, I don't care about what you ate." Ava rested her elbows on her knees. "What was it like? What's *he* like?"

Courtney realized her daughter wanted feelings, impressions, and that was so much more complicated than the basic facts of menu choices. But if this plan was going to succeed, she had to really sell it.

"Well, where do I start?" That was a stall.

"What kind of car does he have?"

"It's a sporty two-passenger Mercedes. One of the pricey ones, I think. Black." The color suited him. There was something dark he carried around when he wasn't making an effort to be charming. And the style of his luxury vehicle revealed a lot. It wasn't a family car. "The seats are leather."

"So you can check off the nice-car box." Ava's look said she was eager for more.

"He opened the door for me." Again, she was a sucker for a gentleman. Recalling that detail gave her a funny little shimmy in the pit of her stomach.

"Cool. And?" the teen prompted.

"First dates are hard." *Especially when it's not a date at all.* "Conversation was awkward at first. But Gabe came to the rescue."

"How?"

"His aunt Lil suggested he bring along the dating profile you filled out for me." She was still wondering why he hadn't destroyed it. There had been a funny look on his face when he used the "too busy" excuse. "And he'd filled out one for himself. We compared notes. It was a really good conversation starter." And very revealing. "That was fun and got us over a little rough patch. It was easy after that."

"What else?" Ava asked.

Courtney racked her brain for details. "He bought dinner."

Ava's delicate brows drew together. "Isn't the guy supposed to pay when he asks you out? That's what you always tell me."

"Right." Shouldn't have been noteworthy, but it was. Because that was another gentlemanly gesture. It came under the heading of *too much information*. "You're the one checking the boxes. Put a mark in that one."

Ava grinned and made a check mark in the air. "Is there chemistry with him?"

"You mean am I attracted?" Courtney was breathing, and he was gorgeous. *Duh.* "I don't want to move too fast. That's the kiss of death."

"Either you are or you aren't." This kid was nothing if not practical—and pushy.

"Well, he's fun. Smart. Great sense of humor. Thoughtful."

"Don't forget cute." Ava shrugged. "For an old guy."

Courtney laughed. "I don't even want to know what that makes me. Ancient, I'd guess."

"I didn't say that." She grinned, then turned serious again. "Do you think he's nice-looking?"

"Yeah, I do." Courtney had thought that the first time they met, when she'd never expected to see him again. Tonight she'd gotten to know him a little better and found out he wasn't just another pretty face. And they had taken a serious step forward in their conspiracy. "And you were right about him, sweetie."

"What did I say?"

"That he was a nice man. Your instincts were spot-on."

The teen smiled, then stood and hugged her. "I'm so glad, Mom. You deserve a nice man."

Courtney returned her hug, then tightened it a little more. "Thank you. It means a lot that you approve of him."

"You make him sound perfect. Smart, funny, thoughtful, cute. You seem really happy. What's not to like?" Ava pointed a finger at her. "Now, don't blow it."

"Okay." That was easy to promise, because she couldn't make a mistake.

"'Night, Mom."

"Sleep tight, sweetie."

Courtney watched Ava leave and blew out a relieved breath. This plan had passed the first test with flying colors. And she realized it was easy, because she'd been telling the truth about Gabe. Fake dating wasn't so hard with someone like him.

Was it a betrayal of their deal that she was looking forward to the next "date"?

Chapter Six

Tuesday and Thursday were Gabe's days to tutor at the high school, an hour at a time—more if there was enough interest. His schedule was posted in the algebra classrooms, and today he was using Brett's. His friend was supervising the math decathlon students.

A couple of kids had wandered in, and he'd given them a few pointers to assist with their homework assignment. It clicked quickly, and they'd left. There was one boy still there. Paul had been a regular since school had started a few weeks ago. He got an A for effort and was doing pretty well in the class. It was just that he lacked confidence in his ability to comprehend the material.

"I don't even know why I have to study algebra."

There was a mother lode of frustration in Paul's voice.

"Well, first it allows us to make statements that are generally true without having to be specific," Gabe began.

"I can be specific." The boy looked up at him. "I specifically hate algebra."

Gabe tried not to laugh and couldn't manage it. He really enjoyed working with the kids and was determined that this one would change his attitude.

"Paul, think of it this way. You can say A plus B equals B plus A rather than five plus three equals three plus five. See, nonspecific but always true."

"Duh." He rested his chin in his hands.

"Also, algebra is a more brief language. It's easier to say 'A plus B equals B plus A' rather than 'when adding two numbers together, it doesn't matter which number is added to which.' The result is still the same."

"Nope." The kid shook his head. "Still not making me care about it."

"Sure you do. Otherwise you wouldn't be here." Gabe saw a girl walk into the classroom at the back. It was Ava. "The last reason algebra is important is you can use it to solve problems."

"No," Paul said, "you can use it. I don't understand it."

"I think you get it more than you think. Why don't you try your homework and we'll go from there."

After heaving a sigh, Paul opened his book and wrote down the first problem. He looked at it for several moments, then started solving it. When he finished, Gabe checked the answer.

"Good job. Keep going."

While Paul worked, Gabe walked to the back of the classroom, where Ava was waiting. "Hi."

She lifted a hand. "What's up?"

"Just tutoring." He rested a hip against an empty desk. "Your mom said you were negotiating more lenient grounding terms and suggested bringing up your math grade for a lighter sentence. Do you need some help with that?"

Her hesitation told him this drop-in had nothing to do with algebra and everything to do with checking him out. He'd gone out with her mother a few days ago, and the reality of that might just be sinking in.

"You're here about your mom and me, right?"

She caught the corner of her lip between her teeth and set her backpack on the desk. "My mom is all about taking responsibility."

"Okay." He had a feeling he knew where this was headed. "What is it you need to take responsibility for?"

"If she gets hurt, it will be my fault."

"Are you asking me not to call your mother for another date?"

Her brown eyes were a swirling mass of confusion and conflict. Finally she blurted out, "Are you going to? Call her, I mean?"

"Yes."

He actually looked forward to seeing her again. The "date" had gone better than he could have anticipated—a lot of laughs and Courtney kept him on his toes. She was quick and obviously intelligent. He was definitely planning to take her out again but was waiting a respectable amount of time. As long as they kept the ruse going, there would be peace and no surprise female guests for him at Blackburne family Sunday dinners.

"Do you like her?" Ava asked.

"Very much." Gabe couldn't have picked anyone more perfect for this mission. It was a plus not having to lie, at least about his feelings for her mother. He couldn't resist asking, "Did she say anything about me?"

Ava smiled a little. "What is this? High school?"

He looked around the classroom and grinned. "Actually, yeah."

"My mom said she had a good time." But Ava didn't look happy about that.

"Hey, Mr. B?"

Gabe turned to look at Paul. "What's up?"

"I finished my homework. But I think it's all wrong. Can you check it out?"

"Of course." He looked at Ava. "Would you excuse me for a minute?"

"I guess."

"I'll be right back." He walked over to the desk where the boy was sitting. Leaning over, he scanned the kid's work and pointed to one of the equations. "This answer is correct, but your teacher wants you to show all the steps. You missed one here."

"What about the rest?"

"Looks good to me." Gabe held out his fist, and the kid bumped it with his own. "You sure complain a lot for someone who really seems to get it."

"That's just part of my process, I guess." He shrugged but looked pretty pleased with himself.

"It's working for you. Anything else you need help with?"

"No." He put his book and paper in his backpack and stood. "Thanks for the help, Mr. B."

"I didn't do anything. It was all you, kid. Keep up the good work."

"See you next time." He headed toward the back of the classroom. "Hi, Ava."

"Hey, Paul." She lifted a hand and looked a little uncomfortable.

"The homework is pretty easy. I didn't think it would be, and this is Mr. B's day to tutor. He's cool."

"Math isn't my favorite," she said, glancing at Gabe.

"Mine, either," Paul answered. "But we don't get a choice."

"That's for sure." She smiled. "See you tomorrow."

"Good luck with the homework." He waved at Gabe. "Later, Mr. B."

"Have a good evening, Paul." Gabe walked back over to Ava and leaned against the desk again. "Okay. So your mom had a good time with me the other night."

"Yeah. She said you have a nice car and were a

gentleman. The conversation was good and you paid for dinner. That's a little old-fashioned, but nice."

Good to know he still had some game in the dating department. "I see."

"She also said you're smart and funny. And cute for an old guy."

"Old?" So much for his game.

She smiled. "That wasn't actually her saying it."

"Ah." But clearly this girl had grilled her mother like raw hamburger. "So she told you it went well. And for some reason that's bothering you. Would you like to talk about it?"

She wouldn't quite meet his gaze, so that was a no. Then the words started pouring out. "You seem like a really nice man."

"Your mom said you told her you felt comfortable with me. And that's why you came to Make Me a Match. I appreciate the vote of confidence."

"No problem." She shifted her weight from one foot to the other. "But, the thing is, I'm the one who pushed my mom into going out, and what if—" She caught her bottom lip between her teeth again.

"What if she gets hurt?" he asked gently.

"Yeah. I'm not saying you're a jerk," she added quickly. "But she hasn't had the best experiences. I get why dating is hard for her. I just want her to be happy, you know?"

"I completely understand." He and Courtney had agreed their happy place was being left alone, but their respective families felt the need to butt in. And he couldn't say any of that without revealing his deal with Courtney. However, with their pact in place, he could sincerely reassure this girl that he wouldn't hurt her mother. Gabe was nothing if not a problem solver.

"Look, Ava, I like your mother. We really did have a good time. The truth is that neither of us is looking for anything serious right now." Not ever, as far as he was concerned.

"But what if she gets serious about you and you don't feel the same about her?" Worry darkened her eyes. "You might not mean to hurt her, but she will be anyway."

"That's what dating is all about," he said. "There are no guarantees, no matter how much you want one."

Life had a way of throwing curveballs. He'd never expected his wife to die. She had been young and healthy, with her whole life ahead of her. The familiar heat of anger burned inside him, but he pushed it down. He hadn't been able to control what happened to Margo, but he could control his feelings from now on. And make sure pain like that never touched him again.

"Look, Ava, you're not responsible for what happens with me and your mom. Any more than Make Me a Match is responsible when the two people we bring together don't hit it off."

"But still—"

"Your mom is one of the strongest women I've ever met. She's beautiful, bright and funny. It wasn't smooth sailing the other night, but by the end of the evening, I'd give us a solid A minus." He had to take off points for wanting to kiss her, but that was only a blip. It was gone now. Under control. "Things will work out however they're going to, but it's never a good idea to borrow trouble."

"I can't help it," she said.

"I promise you that I will always be honest with your mother. Right now we're having fun, and that's the most important thing."

"I guess." She didn't look convinced. "But now that I pushed her into it, I'm afraid you're way out of her league."

If anything, Courtney was too good for a guy like him who put his career above everything, even the wife who'd loved him. But saying so wouldn't reassure Ava. And he couldn't tell her what was really going on.

"I'm just a regular guy, kid. Your mother is way above my pay grade." He smiled. "You'd understand if you could see my family. I have two brothers and a sister. They cut me down to size on an annoyingly regular basis. Every Sunday, in fact."

And that gave him an idea. Ava needed to see he wasn't all that. He still had to take this charade out for a spin with his family to convince them he was going out with Courtney. Why not kill two birds with one stone at a Blackburne Sunday dinner?

Go big or go home. Or, in this case, go home and go big.

Receiving doctor's orders on a new cardiac patient had pushed Courtney's lunch back later than usual, and she was starving. She grabbed a food tray, checked out the day's menu and decided on a big salad. There were hospital employees and visitors also buying food, but it wasn't lunchtime-crush busy now. After paying the cashier, she scanned the cafeteria and was pleased and surprised to see her best friend, Taylor Russo, who worked in the neonatal intensive care unit. Now she wouldn't have to eat alone.

She headed to the table in a back corner and set down her tray. "Hey, Tay."

"Courtney! Hi." The green-eyed blonde grinned with pleasure.

"How are things in the NICU?" She poured dressing on the greens piled high with turkey and hard boiled egg and started to toss it.

"Always hectic. But the babies…" She sighed dreamily. "I love it in there."

"So, when are you going to have one?" Courtney knew the answer but asked anyway. It was what she always did.

"As soon as I find a man who appreciates me for the goddess that I am." She chewed a bite of her sandwich and looked thoughtful. "Or I might just have a baby on my own."

"Really? You've given up on finding a man?" Courtney had been about to eat a forkful of lettuce and stopped halfway to her mouth. She'd met Taylor in nursing school, and they'd clicked right away. They became best friends and were thrilled to find jobs at the same hospital, in their preferred respective fields. "You always swore you wouldn't be like me—you wouldn't do the kid thing by yourself."

"No offense, bestie."

"None taken. No one knows better than me how hard it is being both mom and dad to a child. In a perfect world, every kid would have both. But it's not perfect." No one knew *that* better than Courtney, either. "But I wouldn't trade having Ava, being her mother, for anything. Even when she's at her worst."

Taylor's gaze snapped up. "What has that little angel done now?"

"What makes you think—" Before Courtney finished the thought she got the "because I know you" look. "Okay."

She told Taylor the story of Ava's trip to the matchmaker and the scheme to find her a man.

"That kid is something else." Taylor shook her head then looked wistful. "You're lucky to have someone who loves you that much."

"I know. But what she did is equal parts annoying and sweet."

"Mostly sweet." Her friend popped the last bite of her sandwich into her mouth.

"Easy for you to say. Your child didn't tell a very hot guy that you couldn't get a man on your own and needed assistance."

Taylor's eyes widened. "He was good-looking? Ouch."

"I know, right?" She chewed a bite of salad, because telling her best friend about the fake dating was on the tip of her tongue. It had been her idea to keep the whole thing secret. This woman was very close to Ava, and too much information could be a disaster. "She's finally off restriction for lying to me, not being where she told me she would be. That is just not acceptable."

The cell phone in her scrubs pocket vibrated, and she shifted in her chair to slide it out. She looked across the table at her friend. "Sorry. It might be Ava." Without looking at caller ID, she swiped the screen to answer. "Hello?"

"Hi, Courtney. It's Gabe."

She knew his voice, and the skip of her heart was proof that she knew it. Plus her cheeks grew flushed. She could feel the heat. "Hi."

"I had a couple minutes and wanted to leave a voice mail. I didn't expect you to answer. Is this a bad time? Are you at work?"

"No and yes. I'm at lunch right now."

"I'll let you go, then. Sorry to bother you. This can wait."

"That's okay. I can talk. What's up?" She took another bite of food while she listened.

"I don't know if Ava mentioned it, but I saw her at school yesterday. It was my day to tutor, and she came by the classroom."

"Oh good. She's getting math help." And hadn't said a single word about it.

There was a short silence on his end of the line. "Not exactly."

"I don't understand." Courtney put her fork down in her half-eaten salad. "What's going on?"

"She wanted to talk to me."

"About what?"

"She has mixed feelings about pushing you to date. Now that you are, she's afraid you're going to get hurt."

True to her personality, that child was being annoyingly sweet. "So she warned you?"

"Not exactly. It was more that she wanted reassurance about my intentions."

"Oh, Gabe, I'm sorry."

"Don't be. I told her she has nothing to worry about, and that's true," he said.

"Yeah. Pretty much guaranteed." She glanced at Taylor, who was giving her acutely curious looks.

"But it gave me an idea," he continued. "She needs to see that I'm a regular guy. And I need to introduce you to my family sooner rather than later. They know about our dinner and are starting to ask when they get to meet you."

"Oh God—" The mere mention of meeting his family made her appetite disappear.

"Don't panic," he said reassuringly. "It was going to happen sometime so they know I'm not making you up."

Some other time, maybe in the next century, would have been better. When she'd known him a little longer. "I don't know about that."

"It's just Sunday dinner."

"Who will be there?" she asked.

"Just my sister."

The one who worked here at the hospital. "And?"

"My two brothers, one married with twins and another baby on the way. It's a lot, but I think it would be good for Ava. She thinks I'm out of your league."

"What? That little—"

"She's just concerned." There was amusement in his voice. "So, what do you think about you and Ava coming to Sunday dinner at my parents'?"

"You've thought this through? You really think it's necessary?"

"Yes. Although if you don't want to, I can show them photos of us. But meeting you in person will go a long way toward convincing them to stop fixing me up."

Courtney thought for a moment and sighed. "Fair is fair. You had to face Ava. The least I can do is return the favor."

"For what it's worth, I'm confident you can handle it," he said.

She wasn't so sure about that. There were a lot of people in his family, but no guts no glory. "Okay. I'll check with Ava. Unless she has serious problems with the idea, count us in."

"Great. I'll call you later to finalize the details. Sorry to bother you at lunch. Enjoy it. 'Bye."

There was quiet on the other end of the phone, but one look at her friend's face told her the silence at this table was about to end. There would be no enjoying lunch now. "So, that was Gabe."

"And he is?"

"The hot guy Ava told that I couldn't get a man. Gabriel Blackburne. He works at Make Me a Match.

And tutors math at her high school. His best friend is head of the math department there." And she forced herself to stop babbling before it looked as if she had something to hide.

"And why would Ava be warning him off? Are you going out with him?" *And didn't tell me*, her friend's slightly hurt tone said.

"Yes. No. Sort of."

"What does that mean?" Taylor demanded. "And he had to face Ava, so you're going to return the favor. What's going on with you?"

Courtney was backed against the wall and conflicted. What else was new? She and Gabe had agreed that no one else could know the truth of their conspiracy because there was a big risk of it blowing up in their faces. But she told her friend everything and had since the first day they'd met. That's what BFFs did. Not sharing was breaking a fundamental female friendship rule.

"How do I say this?" she started.

"Oh my gosh, you're pregnant." Taylor put one hand over her mouth.

"Dear God, no! Don't even say something like that out loud."

"You're married? Eloped?"

"No." Courtney put up a hand to stop the guessing when her friend started to talk again. "It's nothing that exciting. And I'm telling you this under cone of silence. You cannot say a word about this to anyone. Especially Ava. Promise me."

Taylor made a cross over her heart. "I swear on my future child's life."

"Okay." She took a deep breath. "Gabriel and I are fake dating."

Taylor's mouth shut for a moment. It didn't last long. "You're what now?"

"We are 'going out.'" She put air quotes around the two words. "He's a widower, and his well-intentioned but pushy family is on his case to get back out there. Once too often they threw a woman at him. Ember was the last straw."

"Ember? Seriously?" Taylor smiled. "I'm getting a mental picture. One burning ember, and someone's hair is on fire."

"That's not far from the truth. He just wants them to stop. And I told you what Ava did. She could have turned to the internet and ended up in a very bad place."

"You're not wrong."

"So we commiserated about our shared family issues, and he came up with the idea to pretend to date so everyone will be happy."

"Everyone but you and Gabe."

"Well, he's not hard to take, and that makes me happy." His deep voice had sent tingles everywhere and made her hormones come to attention and salute. But she was keeping that detail to herself. And she'd been sort of eagerly anticipating their next "date." But that was when she'd expected it to be just the two of them for a movie. Maybe dinner again. Not dinner with his family. An audience for their deception hadn't occurred to her.

"What's wrong?" Taylor asked. "Besides the fact that you're fibbing to your child. Do as I say, not as I do. Are you going to put yourself on restriction?"

Courtney winced at the directness. "You're right. I'm a hypocrite. But it seemed like a good idea at the time. And she will never know that it wasn't ever real. We will 'see' each other for a while, then at a mutually agreed-upon time, we'll break up. I'll be disappointed that things didn't work out, and so will he. That will buy us some time before they start in again."

"Sounds like the plan isn't quite working out, though," Taylor said.

"She's worried about him hurting me."

"Ditto. But I always am. Why is she concerned and how does he know about it?"

Courtney explained about Gabe's tutoring, his talk with Ava and her apprehension that he was out of her league. Since meeting his family was eventually part of the strategy, including Ava might relieve her anxiety. "The problem is that now I have to fake date, face-to-face, with his brothers, sister and parents."

"Oh, what a tangled web we weave…" Taylor stopped and sipped her iced tea.

"Wrong thing, right reason," she defended. "And I would appreciate it if you'd stop reminding me that I'm not telling the truth. You're my friend, and I need you."

"Okay." Taylor was serious now. "What can I do?"

"This is a problem. It's one thing to pretend with Ava for a few minutes and walk out the door to go to dinner. It's his family. The people who know him best in the world. Even if I stick to the truth as much as possible, they're liable to see right through me."

The other woman tapped her lip thoughtfully for a moment. "Well, the way I see it, you have two choices."

"I figured there was only one, so that's an improvement." Courtney took a breath. "Please continue."

"You can brazen it out and hope for the best to keep your daughter from driving you to crazy town." She paused for effect. "Or you can come clean."

Courtney thought that over for several moments and shook her head. "Neither option is very good."

"Talk it through," Taylor encouraged.

"If I come clean, what kind of role model does that make me?"

"Wrong thing, right reason," her friend reminded her. "I couldn't resist teasing you, but I really do get that you're doing it out of love for Ava."

"Thanks." She smiled. "I'm glad you understand where I was coming from."

"And in support of faking it," Taylor continued, "you said he's hot, and it sounds like he's charming. So how hard can pretending be?"

After dinner the other night, Courtney realized it wasn't very darn hard. They'd had a good time. "I really hate having to do what I'm doing. But I suppose it's my penance. If I hadn't married a jerk, I would still be with him and Ava wouldn't be so stubborn about this. She thinks I would be with someone now if it wasn't for her and doesn't want me to be alone when she goes to college in a couple years. I don't think I ever realized how much that awful choice I made affected her."

"And now you're still paying the price." Her friend's voice was gentle.

"Big time." There was no point in pretending otherwise. "And this was all Gabriel's idea to keep his family from driving *him* to crazy town."

"So you're going to roll with the pretense?"

"Yes. I know this is going to sound ironic coming from a fraud like myself, but I gave him my word, and I need to hold up my end of this bargain. Except for the part where I spilled the beans to my best friend."

Taylor studied her closely. "Is it possible you're looking forward to this a little bit?"

"You're not wrong. The truth is I like him, but he's just a friend. That's all."

Every cloud had a silver lining, and spending time with Gabe was hers. She might as well enjoy the fun while it lasted. Hopefully dinner with his relatives would fall into the fun zone.

Chapter Seven

Gabe felt a little like a teenager again borrowing his dad's car. His Mercedes was classic and sporty but not big enough to accommodate more than two people. For a loner like himself, that wasn't a problem. For his current situation, it was. So he'd swapped with his dad and was now driving a small SUV. Plus, when he went to trade vehicles, he'd made sure there was no Ember to ambush him by warning his mom that there would be two more for dinner. It was last minute, but she always made enough food for a small country. And she was excited to meet Courtney and Ava.

He had insisted on picking them up because he knew how nervous Courtney was. After parking the car in front of her building, he walked up the gently curving sidewalk to her door, then knocked. While waiting he realized he was very much looking forward to seeing them. Both of them.

The door opened, and Ava stood there smiling. "Hi."

"You look pretty."

"Thanks." She glanced down at her dark jeans and tugged at the hem of her pink T-shirt. "You think this is okay?"

"A little formal for my family," he teased.

She looked unsure. "Should I change?"

"I was kidding. You look perfect."

"Okay." She glanced over her shoulder. "Come on in. Mom will be down in a minute. She's obsessing about her appearance. Must be genetic."

"I'm sure she'll be fine."

"That's what I told her."

"It's just my family," he said.

"I told her that, too." She shrugged. "Didn't help."

"She'll find out when she gets there. And so will you. They're going to love you both."

Gabe wouldn't worry about introducing Courtney to his family even if he had an emotional investment in this relationship. She was beautiful. Down-to-earth and fun. If he worried about anything, it was that his brother Dominic would make a move.

Jealousy sliced through him, just a quick flash of something he hadn't felt in a very long time. But it got his attention. Odd that in his dating years he'd never worried about his brother hitting on women he brought home. Maybe it had something to do with the fact that Dom was between relationships right now. Or the feeling could be about not wanting Courtney exposed to anything uncomfortable because he'd talked her into this agreement. It couldn't be about any deep feelings since said agreement covered all of that. And he was being stupid. Dom was a stand-up guy. Gabe wasn't even sure why the thought had crossed his mind.

"Can I get you anything to drink?" Ava asked.

"Is your mom going to be so long that I'm in danger of dehydrating while waiting?" As far as he was concerned, she could pull her hair into a ponytail and wear a burlap sack. She'd still be gorgeous.

"No. She's ready," Courtney said, on her way down the stairs. "And talking about herself in the third person. That's how nervous she is." When she stood in front of him, she wasn't smiling.

But she was gorgeous. And that was an understatement. Her cream-colored sweater set, jeans and flats were the perfect meet-the-folks clothes. And she *had* pulled her hair into a ponytail, but it was a little off center, with a few curls loose around her face. Simple gold hoops in her ears completed the outfit.

"You look great," he said.

"I hope you're not lying." She twisted her fingers together nervously. "It would be cruel to lead me on when you really think I look like something the cat yakked up."

"I promise I'm being sincerely honest. My actual thought was that you're wearing the absolute perfect meet-the-folks outfit. You look fantastic."

"Now she's just fishing for compliments," Ava said. "Everyone loves you, Mom. Just be yourself."

"I'd rather be anyone but me right now," Courtney mumbled.

Gabe appreciated her honesty. He met her gaze and said, "Listen to the kid. She's wise beyond her years."

"Yes, she is." Courtney looked at her daughter and nodded. "Shall we go?"

"I vote yes," Ava said. "I can't wait to see how we're all going to fit in the Benz."

"Way ahead of you, kid. I have taken care of that," he said a little smugly. "Let's roll."

He walked outside with Ava while Courtney locked up. At the curb sat the practical little SUV. "I borrowed my dad's car."

Courtney's teasing smile momentarily erased the nerves from her expression. "Like a teenager."

"Kind of feels that way." There was no mistaking the disappointment on Ava's face. "I promise you a ride at another time," Gabe told the girl.

"I'm going to hold you to that," the teen said.

They got in, and he drove to his parents' house, located about ten minutes away. There weren't any other cars parked outside besides the Mercedes and cars that belonged to his mother and sister which meant that he was the first to arrive. Considering Courtney's nerves, that was probably a good thing. She wouldn't have to walk into a crowd of Blackburnes and feel as if they were all judging her.

Gabe led them up the walkway to the covered

porch. He knocked once then opened the door. On Sunday it was always unlocked. "Hello."

"Hey, Gabe." His father met them in the entryway and held out his hand, then pulled him into a hug. Then he smiled at the two ladies. "This must be Courtney and Ava."

"Yes." He smiled at both of them and said, "This is my father, John Blackburne."

Courtney shook his hand, and her own was trembling slightly. "It's a pleasure to meet you, Mr. Blackburne."

"Please, call me John."

Gabe looked at his father objectively, the way Courtney and Ava might. The man's hair was silver and made him look distinguished. His blue eyes were friendly and glowed with approval. Nothing scary there.

"Come in. Let's find your mother, Gabe." He settled his hand lightly on Courtney's back to walk beside her. "My son says you work at Huntington Hills Memorial Hospital."

"Yes, sir. I'm a cardiac care nurse."

"My daughter, Kelsey, works in the ER. And my son, Mason, is a doctor there."

"Gabe mentioned that. It's a big place. There are a lot of employees. I don't think I've met either of them."

"You will today." At the end of the hall, he turned left into the kitchen. "Look who's here, honey."

Flo was at the stove stirring a big pot of spaghetti sauce. At the island in the center of the room, Kelsey was cutting up vegetables for a salad. Both stopped working and looked at the newcomers.

"Mom, Kelse, I'd like you to meet Courtney Davidson and her daughter, Ava."

With a fixed smile on her face, Courtney moved closer and held out her hand in greeting. "Nice to meet you, Mrs. Blackburne."

"That's way too formal. It's Florence. Or better yet, Flo." She smiled at Ava. "Welcome. We're so glad to have you."

His sister finished slicing a cucumber. "You look familiar, Courtney."

"So do you." Her brows drew together in thought. "I don't get down to the ER, but probably our paths have crossed in the cafeteria."

"I'm sure that's it." Kelsey nodded. "If I wasn't working in emergency, my second choice would be the cardiac observation unit. I like the challenge and keeping busy."

"Me, too."

"We sent a patient up to your unit the other day. An older man, retired. Tall with a quirky sense of humor."

"I know who you mean." Courtney smiled.

"How's he doing?"

"Pretty well." She looked apologetic. "I can't say more because of privacy issues."

"I get it," his sister assured her.

"Physically he keeps himself in shape, so that worked in his favor. The doctor admitted him for observation out of an abundance of caution."

"That's good." Kelsey tossed lettuce and vegetables together in a big bowl. "I'm sure you feel it up in the unit, too, but there are just certain patients I connect with instantly."

Courtney nodded. "I know what you mean."

"How old are you, Ava?" his mother asked.

"Fourteen. I'm a freshman at Huntington Hills."

"Gabriel tutors math there," his dad interjected.

"I know." The teen smiled shyly. "I've seen him at school."

"How did you and Courtney meet?" Flo asked him.

"Kelsey didn't tell you?"

"No." She grinned at her daughter. "I'll have a word with her about that later."

He looked down at Courtney and recognized uncertainty and a little bit of anxiety in her eyes. This was skirting fake-dating territory, but nothing succeeded like the truth.

"Actually, Ava brought us together." He explained that their first meeting was at the freshman career day event and told them about his Q and A session, when he'd mentioned Make Me a Match. "Ava came into the office to find out about using our dating service for her mother. She had her babysitting money saved up and everything. Courtney came in to pick her up."

His mom gave the teen an "aw" look. "That is so darn sweet of you, Ava."

"I know, right?" Ava looked at her mom, and there

was a "told you so" expression in her eyes. "Would you believe she grounded me?"

"She's leaving out a lot," Courtney said wryly.

"I figured that." Flo gave her a knowing look. "I suspect it's somewhere closer to her heart was in the right place, but execution of the plan crossed some lines."

"Exactly," Courtney said enthusiastically. "Thank you."

"I get it. I'm a mother. It isn't for sissies or push-overs." Flo beamed at him. "Maybe Ava is a future Make Me a Match employee."

"She's a romantic, for sure," Courtney said.

"The important thing is that you met. And Gabriel asked you out."

"I did." He smiled, and Courtney returned it, but he was beginning to recognize the emotion that darkened her eyes. It was guilt. "And here we are."

"And we're so glad you are." Flo smiled her happy mom smile, then said to her husband, "John, we need to get drinks for everyone."

"I'm taking orders," he said.

"I'll give you a hand, Dad."

Gabe could see Courtney was relaxing now and helped his father get out glasses and pour. While he was involved with that, Kelsey talked nursing with Courtney. When beverages were distributed, he had a chance to observe his "date." She was talking about all kinds of things with his sister. His dad was in deep conversation with Ava about high school in general and the football team in particular.

His mother took a quick inventory of everyone comfortably occupied, then came to stand next to him in the doorway. "She seems very nice, Gabriel."

"Ava is a great kid."

"I couldn't agree more, but I was actually talking about her mother."

"Yeah, I knew that."

She looked at him expectantly, watching and waiting for more but didn't get it. "You're going to make me work for this, aren't you?"

"That was my plan, yes."

"It wasn't enough I had to deal with the terrible twos and the teen years." She sighed, but the teasing was there in her eyes. "Do you like her?"

"Yes." That was very true.

"Do you see it getting serious?"

"It's still new, Mom." That was also true, but incomplete. A lie of omission? After Ember, he wasn't going to lose sleep over it.

"Are you going to give me anything?"

"We're having fun." Another very true statement.

"I assume that since you brought her to Sunday dinner, you're planning to ask her out again."

"Yes." All part of the plan. It was a bonus that he was looking forward to it.

"Have I told you lately how annoyingly concise you are?"

"It's a gift." He grinned, and she returned it.

There was a knock on the door, followed by it opening. Childish voices drifted to him, then he heard Mason's loud "Hello."

And Sunday dinner was off and running. Twins Charlie and Sarah ran into the room. After being hugged and kissed by their grandmother, they ran straight to Ava. She went down on their level and smiled at the two of them.

Before greeting the new arrivals, his mother leaned over and said quietly, "It makes me very happy that you're going out again."

The words hit him like a sledgehammer to the chest. Oddly enough, the emotion he felt wasn't grief. It was guilt. He'd been so caught up with Courtney and their strategy to deal with the present that he'd given barely a thought to the past. The love he'd lost. The reason he never wanted love again. How could he have done that?

Courtney was having such a good time with the Blackburne family that for a while she forgot it was all fake. After eating salad, spaghetti, meatballs, garlic bread and homemade brownies topped with ice cream, she was in the family room with Gabe's very pregnant sister-in-law, Annie. Her twins were on the floor roughhousing with Ava, and their laughter was hilarious—and contagious. Gabe was standing near the sliding glass door to the backyard with his brothers and father. Flo and Kelsey were in the kitchen finishing the dishes. They flatly refused any help.

Every few minutes, Gabe would look over at her, and she wondered if they were talking about her. She tried not to care whether or not they liked her but couldn't quite pull that off.

"Ava is so good with Charlie and Sarah," Annie said. "Would it be okay if she comes home with us?"

Courtney pulled her focus away from the men and concentrated on her own conversation. "She loves kids. Even has her Red Cross advanced childcare certification."

"Impressive." Annie tucked her long blond hair behind her ears, then rested her hands on her pregnant belly. "And it's a luxury for me to be able to sit back and relax. I usually have to jump up every few minutes and stop them from getting into something they shouldn't or referee their fights."

"I refuse to believe those two adorable, golden-haired angels fight."

"Believe it." Annie laughed. "And being a boy, Charlie is a little huskier than Sarah and takes her toys because he can. We're working on the concept of sharing right now."

"How's that going?"

"Could be better." She sighed. "And when this new baby comes, it's anyone's guess how that will go over."

"It's normal for them to have a reaction. Think about it. Some little intruder is going to steal their mom away. They'll probably act out for attention, but it will pass."

Annie's expression turned playfully serious. "I wasn't kidding about taking Ava home with me."

"Maybe after the baby is born she could come over from time to time and help out so you can give the twins your undivided attention for a while."

"That's a great idea. And I'm happy to pay her."

"I'll talk to her about it." A squeal of laughter from the little guy her daughter was tickling made her smile. "And just think, that would give her more disposable income for hiring a matchmaker for me."

"That story is priceless," Annie said.

And the reason she was here with Gabe. The reminder that this wasn't real hit her hard. When they "broke up," there was a good chance his sister-in-law wouldn't want his ex's daughter babysitting. These people were so awesome, and she was deceiving them. What a horrible person she was!

At that moment, Gabe walked over and held out his hand to her. "Annie, mind if I steal Courtney away for a little while? I want to show her the backyard."

"Is that what you two crazy kids are calling alone time these days?" There was a suggestive tone in her voice, and she winked. "Enjoy the 'tour,' Courtney."

"Thanks."

She put her hand in his and let him pull her up. His palm was wide, warm and strong, and for some reason that made her heart flutter. They walked outside, and before the door closed, there were catcalls and whistles from the boys and sharp warnings from the girls for them to stop being jerks.

Gabe led her to the edge of the covered patio trimmed in brick. He pretended to point out shrubs and flowers that ringed the grass. His arm was casually around her waist and shouldn't feel nice, but it really did.

"I thought we should debrief on how the operation is going so far," he said. "When you were talking to Annie just now, you got a funny look on your face. Are you okay?"

"I was nervous at first," she admitted. "And on my guard."

"I noticed," he said wryly. "Probably that worked in our favor. They'll no doubt figure that you were tense because you like me and wanted to make a good impression."

There was some truth to that, although she could barely admit it to herself, let alone him. "Speaking of impressions, when we first got here, you were talking to your mom and got a look on your face, sort of sad but angry at the same time. What did she say?"

His mouth pulled tight for a moment, and it seemed as if he wasn't going to answer. Finally, he said, "She said she was glad that I was going out again. That made me realize you're the first woman I've brought home to meet the family since my wife died."

"Oh, Gabe—" She felt an overwhelming urge to comfort and leaned her head on his shoulder. "I'm sorry. Now I feel even more awful."

"Why?"

"That's the whole reason we're doing this. To get your family past the firsts and off your back. I've been following your lead, answering questions with the truth—how we met, we're new, not serious. But I let my guard down because they're so nice. Then Annie said something about Ava paying for a matchmaker, and I remembered that I'm playing a part. The idea of faking them out was much easier before meeting everyone. I like them a lot. They're really good people."

"I know."

"But do you?" She stepped away and faced him. It was too hard to say this with his body touching hers. "I don't know if you can really appreciate them and how lucky you are that they care so much. But I do."

"Of course I value them."

"Really?" She shook her head. "I was seventeen and pregnant, and my parents' already failing marriage crumbled. Neither of them wanted me or the 'brat' I was carrying."

"They probably said that in anger. One of them changed their mind?"

"No."

He sighed. "It's just really hard for me to believe that they would completely cut off their daughter."

"That's because you were fortunate enough to be born into your family and they wouldn't treat one of their own that way." The scary, painful memories scrolled through her mind. "I couch surfed and stayed in shelters. After Ava was born, I reached out to my parents, but they didn't want anything to do with us. We have no contact with them. One of the hospital nurses gave me a room. She lived alone and helped me with Ava while I finished high school. She encouraged me to go to college, too, and I worked part-time jobs. She was kind and generous, everything my family should have been. I went into a nursing program because of her."

"Wow, I'm sorry you had to go through that." He looked really angry.

"It is what it is. I don't think about them much anymore. My point is that your family would never have abandoned you like that. They accepted me because they think I'm with you. It makes me feel terrible being here under false pretenses."

"I know better than anyone how great they are, but they're not perfect. This is the first enjoyable Sunday dinner I've had in a long time, because I got to choose the woman I sat beside."

"You're welcome." She gave him a small smile.

"I love them very much, but their interference is making me nuts. It has to stop." He dragged his fingers through his hair. "And really, this was the hardest part. It's all downhill from here."

"Oh? And where do we go from here?" she asked.

"Just like we agreed. We convince them we really care about each other so when we 'break up' they will all believe I need time and space to get over you."

"Then they'll just start trying to fix you up again."

"But by then Make Me a Match should be earning a comfortable profit for my aunt. Her retirement will be secure, and my mother can rest easy that her sister will be fine in her golden years."

"What will you do then? Will you stay with the company?" she asked.

"One of the reasons I agreed to help my aunt was

to give myself time to figure out what I wanted. So I've been thinking about it."

"And?" she prodded.

"By the time Make Me a Match is out of the woods, I'll be close to making a decision about starting my own company out of state. Too far away for the Blackburne family to interfere in my life."

That surprised her more than a little. "You're going to leave?"

"I'm a nomad. When I was contracting my services to pull companies out of the cellar, moving around was what we—" He stopped and blew out a breath before meeting her gaze again. "I moved all over the country. My plan always was to stop freelancing and start my own business. In the back of my mind, I was continuously looking for the best place to locate my headquarters."

Well, shoot. Courtney realized she didn't really know him that well, and already what he'd just revealed made a little bit of a dent in her heart. The information shouldn't even be a blip on her emotional monitor, but the revelation definitely produced a spike. His future plans shouldn't matter because they wouldn't be together even if he was still living in Huntington Hills.

That thought made her inquire about something. "I'm curious, though. Obviously your family is thrilled that you're here. You love them," she said. "So, if you can put your company's head office anywhere, why not open it here in town? The industrial center is expanding. Seems to me that would be a win-win."

"What part of 'they are too involved in my personal life' did you not understand?"

"Don't you want to stay here?" She tilted her head and looked up at him. "Think about it. Seems to me the worst that could happen is after we 'break up'—" She added air quotes. "—you could just find another fake date partner."

"I don't know—" He stopped when something in the house caught his attention.

"What?" She looked over and could see most of the Blackburnes standing by the sliding glass door. They were talking and looking out the window. "Are they spying on us?"

"And family interference strikes again. Now do you get it? Just a little?" His expression was apologetic. "They assumed I brought you out here to be alone. And kiss you."

"Maybe they're just hoping?" she suggested. Her cheeks felt hot, and her heart started to pound. "Because we did both tell them we were taking things slow."

"What can I say?" He shrugged. "The thing is, our plan was to really sell us as a dating couple."

"And in that context, a kiss would probably be acceptable. Even with the parameters of taking it slow."

"Even expected," he said. "There's an expression… Show, don't tell."

"Actions speak louder than words." She nodded.

"Are you okay with it?"

Her bubbling hormones were saying *bring it on*. She was more than okay. "Yes. You?"

"Yeah." Was it her imagination that there was eagerness in his voice?

"Then we should probably show them," she said a little breathlessly.

He reached for her hand and pulled her closer, although their bodies didn't touch. "Here goes."

Courtney took that as her cue and quickly leaned forward at the same time he did. Their foreheads banged together.

"Ouch." She reached a hand up to rub her head.

"Sorry. You okay?"

"Fine. I'm not always that clumsy." But she was that embarrassed.

"My fault," he said. "Guess I'm off my game."

She met his gaze and couldn't help smiling. "I guess we really showed them."

"Maybe they didn't notice."

"And maybe I'll click my heels three times and you won't have to drive me home," she teased.

"Yeah. You're right. I'm pretty sure Dominic gave me a thumbs-down. It's official. There's no salvaging that, and I'll never hear the end of it."

"I guess our technique needs work," she said.

"It does if we're really going to make believers out of them." He was still holding her hand and brought it to his lips for a brief kiss. "So I propose a solution. Friday night, dinner and kissing class."

"It's a 'date.'"

Chapter Eight

During her first dinner with Gabe, Courtney had been nervous because she'd never fake dated before. Sunday with the Blackburnes didn't count because she wasn't alone with him. Although her hand still tingled where he'd kissed it. But now it was Friday night and she was in a restaurant, sitting across the table from him. The place was wood beams, white tablecloths and candles. Just elegant enough to be sophisticated, yet comfortable and cozy. Except after this part there would be "kissing class." What did that mean? And how could she so casually have answered "It's a date"? It was casual and easy because she'd air quoted it.

He hadn't yet said anything about tonight's goal. Maybe he'd forgotten about the whole thing.

They'd already ordered drinks and given their food choices to the server, so now it was time to fill the silence with innocuous conversation.

"How was your week?" she asked.

"Good. Our advertising efforts are continuing to pay off. We had a lot of new clients. It's been busy." He took a drink of his beer. "How was yours?"

"Also busy. And not in a good way like you."

"Yeah." He nodded. "When you're busy, it's because people are sick."

"I was glad to have the last couple days off," she admitted.

"And tonight you don't have to cook. That's nice, right?"

"Yes." And no. Because after dinner, class might be in session and she wasn't sure she wouldn't embarrass herself again.

"Are you working this weekend?"

"Yeah."

"That gets you out of Sunday dinner, then," he said.

"I didn't realize I was invited."

"You have an open invitation." He smiled. "My mom is hoping I'll bring you back again."

"That means they didn't hate me."

"Are you kidding?" He shook his head. "They thought you were great."

Courtney wanted very much to ask if he shared the family opinion but held back. For some reason, she just didn't want to hear about being nothing but a means to an end.

"I think they liked my daughter and I'm just getting positive feedback by association."

He grinned, turning his beer bottle. "They loved Ava and want to make her an honorary Blackburne. She fit right in. According to my mom, that's because you must be a fantastic mother."

"Stop, you're making me blush." She wasn't lying about that. "Ava loved them all, too, especially the twins."

"They're pretty cute." Gabe's expression turned serious as he studied her. "You're looking pensive about something. What's on your mind?"

Kissing class. But that could wait. "I feel sad that Ava has never had a traditional family. No grandparents."

"Do you regret not reconciling with your folks?"

She shook her head. "When Ava started asking about them, I got in touch one more time. They're divorced, and we visited each of them. They don't speak to each other, and both of them independently believed the visits were about dumping Ava on them."

"You'd never abandon your child," he said firmly.

"You're right about that. Obviously you know me better than my own parents." She picked up her glass and sipped some of the cabernet. "We don't need that kind of negativity in our life."

"It's their loss."

"Is it really only theirs, though?" She met his gaze. "Ava is missing out on grandparents to spoil her and tell her she's perfect." She looked away for a moment. "And what if she gets attached to your family? When we end this, she could get hurt."

Gabe toyed with the fork on the table and looked thoughtful for a few moments. "I don't have all the answers, Courtney. Wish I did. But I think the scenario you're describing comes under the heading of borrowing trouble. Let's just take this one step at a time."

"Yeah. You're probably right."

If she ended this charade right now, Ava would accuse her of not trying. Being too picky. With Gabe, what was not to like? He checked a lot of the good boxes. But there was one he didn't check—looking for a relationship. His family was happy that he was moving forward, but they didn't know this was all a lie designed to *not* get back in the saddle.

Just then their dinner arrived, and this time they'd both ordered the same thing—a big, juicy steak, medium rare, baked potato and broccoli. The server suggested they cut the meat to make sure it was cooked to their satisfaction, then said simply, "Enjoy your dinner."

After chewing a bite, Courtney said, "This is really good."

"Mine, too." He looked around. "I like this place."

"You've never been here before?"

"No. I think it's pretty new."

"Are you checking it out for Make Me a Match?"

"Not formally. But I'm always looking for new ideas. Sometimes clients ask for recommendations.

I'll keep it in mind. Maybe a promotional change from Patrick's Pub at some point to bring in clients."

In spite of her nerves, Courtney managed to eat half of her dinner and requested a to-go box for the rest. Of course the waiter asked if they'd saved room for dessert, and she said yes. Anything to delay part two of this "date." Again Gabe split it with her—this time a caramel cheesecake.

After taking the last bite, Courtney licked the spoon. "That was so worth it."

"The calories?"

That, too, but she meant a delaying tactic. It was both successful and scrumptious. "Yeah," she said, "the calories."

The check came, and the waiter assured them there was no rush. Courtney couldn't agree more. She wasn't sure what lesson she'd learn in kissing class, but no doubt awkwardness would be involved somehow. And the devil of it was, she really *wanted* to kiss him. That could be part of her problem, because it wasn't part of their agreement.

Her preoccupation was a distraction that gave Gabe an advantage, and he grabbed the check before she could. Again.

"This one was supposed to be mine," she protested.

"Yeah." He shrugged. "About that… Let's call it a thank-you for putting up with my family and pulling the whole thing off successfully."

"Right," she said wryly. "Because they were so darn hard to take."

"They can be intimidating. Just the sheer number of them. And you handled it beautifully." He was looking straight at her, and on the last word, his voice was as dark and smooth as the caramel in the dessert, and his eyes were smoky and exciting.

"Well—okay. Thanks for dinner, then." Her heart tripped, and she sounded a little breathless even to herself.

They walked outside, and he settled his hand at the small of her back, even though there was no one around to pretend for. What was up with that? She wondered about it, at the same time liking the gesture very much. Too soon the valet brought the car around, and Gabe opened the door for her. When she was safely inside, he tipped the guy, then slipped into the driver's seat.

He put on his seatbelt and said, "Where to?"

"Home, I guess."

"It's pretty early," he pointed out. "Won't Ava wonder about that?"

"I do have to work tomorrow."

"But do you turn in this early?" he asked.

"No. I'm a night person. All those years of work, school and raising Ava turned me into one."

"Okay." He pulled out of the parking lot and took a left at the first light.

"So where are we going?"

"My place. Just to kill some time until you can go home at an appropriate hour to avoid suspicion and questions." He glanced over at her, but even the lights from the dashboard didn't illuminate his expression.

"Sounds like a plan."

The drive probably took ten to fifteen minutes but felt like seconds. He lived in a town home complex surrounded by grass, trees, shrubs and sidewalks. There was a security gate and he entered a code, then drove past the various buildings until pulling into a parking space. Inside they took the elevator to the top floor, and he led the way to his unit on the end.

Gabe unlocked the door and said, "Be it ever so humble…"

Courtney walked in and looked around. There was a living room, dining room, wet bar and kitchen with granite countertops and dark cherrywood cabinets. The floor was wood, with expensive-looking area rugs scattered throughout. A stairway to her left indicated another level where the bedrooms probably were located. Straight ahead were floor-to-ceiling windows with a view of the lights in the Huntington Hills valley. It was quite beautiful.

"Nice place." She was a master of understatement.

"Thanks. But I can't take credit. This is a rental."

Besides his two-seat Mercedes Benz, this was another piece of the puzzle that was Gabriel Blackburne. He had zero intention of pursuing a family lifestyle.

She stood in the living room beside the leather corner group. "What are we going to do?"

"I was thinking of opening a bottle of wine. And then we should get comfortable with the things a 'normal' dating couple would do."

He didn't do air quotes, but Courtney could hear

them in his voice. And now she knew he hadn't for-gotten. "You're talking about kissing class."

"Well, we sure didn't sell that to my family. Along with how much they like you, I heard about how bad a kisser I am. My smooth factor was missing in action."

"I was right there with you. Hopefully you men-tioned that while they were taking you down a peg or two."

"Absolutely not. I gallantly shouldered all the blame. As well I should. It was my fault."

"I disagree, but obviously that's a moot point."

"I appreciate you trying to take one for the team, though." He indicated the sofa. "Have a seat. I'll get wine."

"Okay." She removed her jacket and set it on the glass coffee table along with her purse. After a last look at the view, she sat down.

Gabe brought over two glasses half-full of a golden liquid then handed one to her before sitting beside her. Their bodies didn't quite touch, but she could feel the heat from his. He looked so relaxed and handsome in his dark jeans and pale yellow dress shirt. And there was something very sexy about the way the long sleeves were rolled to mid-forearm. Her hormones started bubbling, letting her know how much they approved of where this was going. But she was nervous.

After taking a sip of wine, she met his gaze. "So, I'm going to be honest. It's been a while for me. I haven't really been out with anyone since my marriage broke up, and that was three years ago. That was probably the reason I nearly gave you a concussion at your mom's. My point in telling you this is to explain that I'm a little tense."

"I noticed." He set his wine on the coffee table, then took hers and did the same. "It's been a while for me, too."

She would never have guessed. "How do we do this?"

"We'll start gradually." He thought for a moment then held out his hand. "Slow and simple."

She put hers in his wide palm, and he linked their fingers. "Okay, now what?"

"We'll just do this for a while." His body language appeared relaxed, but he wasn't just going through the motions. Not entirely. His voice was a little ragged, and there was a delicious heat in his eyes.

Courtney instinctively moved closer, sliding sideways until their thighs touched. "And how do you think phase one is going so far?"

"Pretty well." He swallowed hard. "You?"

"F-fine." She could barely speak, her breathing was so shallow.

"Good. Initiating phase two, then." He untangled his fingers from hers and cupped her face in his hands before gently pressing his lips to hers.

They were soft, warm and the tender touch made her go up in flames. She put her hands on his chest and sighed at the contour of muscle beneath his shirt. He groaned, and his breathing escalated. He slid one arm behind her back and the other beneath her thighs and lifted her into his lap, never breaking the contact of their mouths.

He kissed her cheeks, her neck and a sensitive spot near her ear, cranking up the heat. Her fingers found the buttons on his shirt, and she undid one, then another. His hand was at her waist and slid underneath her sweater, rubbing up and down her back. When he touched her breast, a moan was trapped in her throat. She desperately wanted more, wanted him touching her bare skin everywhere. The nerves she'd been rocking disappeared, replaced by overwhelming desire. At that moment, she wanted him more than her next breath.

That thought stopped her cold and made her freeze. This wasn't supposed to happen.

Gabe sensed the change and went still. "Courtney?"

Awkwardly she slid off his lap and turned her back, moving away to get her jacket. She hadn't been prepared for this, mentally or any other way. "I think I need to go."

He didn't say anything for several moments. Finally he let out a long breath and said, "Okay. I'll drive you home."

"Thanks. I'm—" *Sorry* wouldn't cut it.

She heard the strain in his voice, the ragged edges of it, and felt like an idiot. If only the earth would open and swallow her whole. If only she'd been wrong about the awkwardness factor. Unfortunately, she'd managed to humiliate herself again.

* * *

Five days later, Gabe still couldn't get that kiss off his mind. Too many times to count, he'd found himself staring into space and seeing Courtney's face, her lips parted, chest heaving and a shocked expression in her eyes. The consuming need he'd felt had been totally unexpected. He didn't know what to say to her, and she'd been very quiet after telling him she needed to leave.

Later the anger hit him, familiar and fierce. Wanting Courtney so badly felt like a betrayal of the wife he'd sworn to love forever. That night he hadn't thought about Margo at all. Not until he'd returned to his empty condo and saw her photo on the end table, beside the couch where he'd nearly had sex with Courtney.

"Damn it. The ground rules should have included what to do about sex." He slammed his desk drawer shut.

"Knock, knock." Aunt Lil stood in the doorway. "Can I come in? Or are you still busy venting? Yes, I've noticed. So has Carla."

"It's fine. Have a seat." With an effort, he pushed the anger away and forced a smile as she sat in one of the club chairs. The concerned expression on her face was a clue that his heated outburst would not be ignored. "What's up? I thought you went home for the day."

"No. I was about to head out right after Carla left, but I got a phone call."

He noted the change in her expression—in a good way. "I say again. What's up?"

"Do you remember Nicole and Dan?"

He thought for a moment. "Sounds familiar, but I can't quite pull the information from my memory banks."

"If only you could get your head out of the iCloud." Her grin was just a little wicked.

"Very funny, Aunt Lil."

"I think so. You young people are so smug about your superior computer skills, but don't forget who taught you how to use a spoon."

"That will never happen," he assured her. "Not with you and my mom around to remind me."

"Okay then." She had an "I told you so" look on her face that had nothing to do with computers or puns. "Nicole and Dan are the first match you and I disagreed about when you came to work here. You thought she had no distinctiveness, too bland. And he was a blowhard jerk."

"Okay. Yeah. You thought she needed time to come out of her shell and would be the perfect complement to his big personality. I remember now."

"Well, he just called with the good news. He proposed, and she accepted. He was very grateful. And humble," she added.

This conversation made Gabe cautiously optimistic that she would overlook his fit of temper. He so didn't want to talk about the reason for it and might just get out of this without a chat. "Wow, I can't believe they're engaged."

"Believe it. You scoffed and mocked me, but my instinct is taking on legendary proportions. And I say that with all humility."

"Yeah, I noticed." He didn't hold back the sarcasm. With her he didn't have to. "I would not have put money on those two making a match."

"Oh, ye of little faith. When are you going to listen to me?"

"From now on," he promised, then realized his mistake. He should have qualified his answer and made it just about her business.

"Then, as they say, I'm going to strike while the iron is hot." Now her concerned look was back. "Are you and Courtney having an issue?"

"Why would you ask that?"

"Correct me if I'm wrong, but did we not just talk about my relationship instincts being right on?"

"We did, but Nicole and Dan are strangers, which is why your gift is so remarkable. Family is quite a different thing." It sounded moronic even to him, but he was going to defend the position until hell wouldn't have it.

"You are so wrong." She crossed her legs and gave him a pitying look. "And this is me. I took you under my wing. You were such a quiet, sensitive boy and got even more quiet when your mother was on bed rest during her last pregnancy. You needed attention, and with everything going on, you were overlooked. But I saw."

"You did." Gabe loved that about her—at the same

time, he hated this conversation and where it was going. "Do we really have to talk about this?"

His aunt stared at him as if she could see his thoughts. "I'm sensing your frustration."

He took that as a yes. "Really? I don't know why."

"Maybe because you said something about sex before slamming your desk drawer."

"Well, crap." He'd been hoping she hadn't heard that.

"I might be old as dirt, but there's nothing wrong with my hearing."

"You are ageless and beautiful, inside and out." He sincerely meant that.

"And you are a shameless flatterer. I love you for it, Gabriel." She sighed. "And don't think I'm not aware that you're trying to distract me. It won't work."

"Bummer."

That got a smile, but it was fleeting. "Something happened with you and Courtney."

"I will neither confirm nor deny."

"Lovable nephew turns into stubborn, infuriating man," she said almost to herself. "Something happened to put you in a mood. Just tell me about it."

Courtney had shut down the kiss and couldn't get away fast enough. At first he'd been relieved, partly because his anger had come back. It was trusty and familiar. Nothing got through when his old friend anger was firmly in place. But it was nowhere to be found when he really needed it—when he'd kissed Courtney and gave in to the wanting. One touch of his mouth to hers shut down common sense, and he couldn't keep his hands off her. He'd been kicking himself ever since.

The thing was, she'd gone radio silent and it felt over. He didn't want things with Courtney to be over. He needed more time. Time to convince his family it would take more than a couple of weeks to get over her. That had been the mission's objective. And he'd built an impressive business reputation on achieving objectives.

"I'm not sure what's going on," he finally said.

"How does Courtney feel?"

"I haven't talked to her."

"How do you feel?" his aunt asked.

"Like I need to talk to her."

The older woman stood and looked down at him. "Then I suggest you do that."

Gabe watched her walk to the door. "Aunt Lil?"

She stopped and looked back. "What?"

"Thanks for the pep talk." And for always noticing him, he added silently.

"It wasn't much, but you're so very welcome." She smiled fondly, then met his gaze without flinching. "And for what it's worth, Margo would want you to move on with your life and be happy."

Before he could respond to that, she was gone, and he sighed. His dead wife might want him to be happy, but that was something he didn't believe would ever happen for him again. And he didn't want it to.

Gabe did a little more computer work, then left the office. On the way to his rented condo, he went

to the drive-through and picked up a chicken dinner for one. When he finally walked into his place,
it was after seven. The sound of silence greeted him,
followed by a wave of loneliness with a brutal under-
tow that threatened to sweep him in a direction he
didn't want to go. It was a familiar feeling but had
turned deeper and darker since the night Courtney
had been here.

He set his chicken meal on the kitchen island then
took out his cell phone. After pulling up his contacts,
he tapped Courtney's number and waited. It rang a
few times, and he expected to get voice mail, but
someone answered.

"Courtney Davidson's phone."

"Hi, Ava." He sounded disgustingly cheerful. Just
like a guy who'd almost had sex on his couch with
her mom. "How's math treating you?"

"It sucks." She sounded like a resentful teen who
knew what he'd done.

"Can I help?" Still with the too-cheery voice.

"You can help by telling me what happened with
you and my mom."

"She hasn't said anything?" he asked hesitantly.

"No. But she's been acting weird. What's going
on?"

Delete cheerful tone here. "I'm not going to lie
to you, Ava."

"Right," she said sarcastically.

"I might have messed up with your mom," he said.

"How?" The tone was hostile, and he preferred
sarcasm.

He had no intention of giving her details. "I just need to talk to your mom. Is she home?"

"She's pouring spaghetti into the colander."

"Okay. I'll wait. But will you tell her it's me?"

There was silence for several moments, long enough for him to wonder if she really would do as requested. Then he heard her say, "Mom, Mr. B is on the phone."

There were several more long moments before someone spoke. "Gabe?"

"Hi, Courtney." He blew out a breath then asked, "Are you speaking to me?"

"Of course."

"Okay. Good." He felt like an awkward teen, not sure what to say next. "It's just after the other night— I wasn't sure if you—" He blew out a breath. "I don't know exactly what happened."

"Yeah. Hang on. I'm going into the other room. Ava, will you toss the salad for me?" There was silence on her end for a couple of beats, then she said, "Okay. I can talk now."

"I just wanted to check in. See how you are."

"Honestly? I'm still in recovery from the intensity of that kiss. I didn't expect that with you."

So he wasn't the only one who'd felt it. For a split second that pleased him, then he shut down the feeling. "But we're friends."

"I've never done that with a friend." There was astonishment in her voice.

"I have to ask. Should I apologize?"

"Absolutely not," she said vehemently. "It just

took me by surprise, that's all. We were practicing to make it look real, and mission accomplished. When the hormones took over, it got real."

"Right. So, I have to ask. Do you want to call things off?" *Please say no*, he thought. He hadn't been sure about moving forward with this when talking with his aunt, but he was now. He definitely was not ready to end things yet.

"I don't. Do you?"

"No," he said. "But where do we go from here?"

"Well, I think kissing class gets an A plus. We now know we can make it look real." She hesitated for a moment, then cleared her throat. "I wanted to go for it with you. I want to continue our agreement because it's working, but I need to be smart and safe. I need to visit my doctor and have a serious discussion about birth control."

Gabe couldn't help smiling. It was sincere amusement along with profound respect for her blunt, straightforward comment and all it implied. For the first time in a very long time, he was going to have sex.

"I think that's a very good idea," he said.

"Right. Let's be clear. This isn't love. But with what happened the other night, I think we can say that there's a definite attraction. And we agreed this would be fun. Sex is fun, but it's best to be prepared and take precautions. More than a condom."

"Absolutely." He was glad this wasn't FaceTime, because she would see that he was grinning from ear to ear.

"Okay. I have to go. Ava just walked into the room, and she's got that look on her face that says she's hungry."

"Okay. I'll call you soon."

"I look forward to it. 'Bye, Gabe."

He tapped the red stop button on his phone and put it down beside his dinner for one. His appetite had returned with a vengeance. Suddenly he was hungry and had a feeling it wasn't just about food. Feelings stirred inside him but he understood they were, as Courtney had said, hormones. That explained his sudden change in feelings. He was a guy and he liked her. He also liked sex, and it had been a hell of a long time. Neither of them was looking for anything serious. They could have fun with no worries about the future. That's all this was.

Chapter Nine

"Are you sure you want to come with us?" Courtney carried her coffee over to the little kitchen table and set it down before sitting in the chair near her daughter's.

Ava finished chewing a bite of cereal, but her eyes were saying, "Are you kidding me?" When she swallowed, she elaborated with words. "Mom, it's the zoo! You said Mr. B invited me to go along. Did he change his mind or something?"

"No, sweetie."

Between her hands she cradled her favorite mug, the one that had the words *World's Best Mom* written on it. Courtney felt like a fraud on so many fronts, but particularly that one. Excluding her current situation with Gabe, Courtney had made it a point to tell her daughter the truth. She'd explained in the gentlest possible terms that Adam Nelson, the jerk she'd had the bad judgment to marry, wanted kids, but only if they were his kids, with his DNA. When he proposed, he'd said he wanted to be a father to Ava but he lied and her daughter had been hurt.

After that she was more determined than ever to protect her child. She didn't believe Gabe would deliberately hurt Ava, and it was really nice of him to include her in today's outing. But she could be collateral damage in this scheme if they weren't careful.

Let's try this again, Courtney thought. "I'm concerned about you, Ava. You could get attached to Gabe after spending time with him. There are no guarantees that he and I will be anything more than friends."

"He's my friend, too, so I don't think it's a problem." Ava took another spoonful of cereal and started to chew.

Courtney was trying to put a finer point on this warning without tipping her hand. "I don't want you to be caught in the middle if there's a nasty breakup because things take a turn."

Like sex. Just the thought of it made her girl parts tingle.

Ava was staring at her. "Why are you being this way?"

"What way?"

"So negative. You don't have an open mind about dating at all. And you always tell me I have to change my attitude. Well, back at you, Mom. It's like you're going into this with an exit strategy."

Wow, since when did this child get so observant? "I just want you to have realistic expectations. This isn't a cartoon fantasy where we know each other for fifteen minutes and live happily ever after."

Ava glared. "So, you're already convinced that things won't work out."

Courtney was absolutely certain of it, because neither she nor Gabriel was looking for love. But she was on very thin ice here. "I just want you to be prepared."

"You mean like our earthquake supplies?" the teen asked.

"If the big one hits, you'll be very thankful to have something to eat," Courtney defended. "And yes, that's what I mean. Hope for the best, prepare for the worst. Just in case."

"Do you like Mr. B at all? Or are you just going out with him because I was on your case?"

The thin ice just cracked, and Courtney was about to fall in. She and Gabe as a legitimately dating couple was a lie, but a face-to-face falsehood offended her maternal code of ethics. It was splitting hairs on the honesty front, but wrong thing, right reason was her defense, and she was sticking to it. She seized on the only question she could answer honestly.

"I like him very much. He's capable of deep feelings."

It was a wonderful quality. Unfortunately all those feelings were for the wife he'd lost. It was a shame that a man like him wasn't willing to put himself out there again. But who was she to point fingers? She was doing the same thing.

"Okay, then." Ava nodded. "Just give him a chance, Mom. Do you think you can do that?"

Courtney put a hand in her lap and crossed her fingers. "Yes. And he's going to be here any minute to pick us up. Finish eating and go brush your teeth. I can't believe I let you have sugar-coated cereal."

Grinning, Ava stood and pointed to the mug. "Because you're the world's best mom."

"Right," she scoffed. "Now scoot."

"I hope he brings the Mercedes." This child had perfected a wickedly teasing expression.

"So, you're not going after all?" Courtney teased back.

Laughing, the teen put her bowl in the sink then ran upstairs. Courtney washed up the dishes, then paced nervously as she waited for Gabe to arrive. She was a little uneasy about how very much she was looking forward to seeing him. And a lot uneasy about Ava coming along.

It was one thing to spend time at his parents' with all the people around for a distraction. Especially the twins. But today it was just the three of them. Could she and Gabe actually pull this off?

They were about to find out.

And then the doorbell rang. Courtney blew out a breath before answering it.

"Hi," she said.

"You ready?"

"Yes. And Ava will be down in a minute. Come in." She stepped back to let him pass and sighed as the masculine scent of his cologne drifted by.

"How are you?" he asked.

"Good. You?"

"Fine." He met her gaze, and there was a smoky sort of look in his eyes for a second. "Feels like I haven't seen you for a long time."

"A couple of weeks, I guess." She knew it had been exactly long enough to see her doctor and be on the pill for a sufficient length of time to not get pregnant. If they did the deed.

There was understanding in his eyes along with a glitter of heat that quickly disappeared. "I can't believe you've never been to the zoo."

She was glad he'd changed the subject. "What can I say? Disadvantaged childhood."

"I'm sorry, Court. Didn't mean to remind you of the bad stuff."

"No problem." She waved away the apology. "It's in the past."

"Is it?"

But just then footsteps sounded on the stairs as Ava came down. "Hey, Mr. B."

"Hi, kid. So you're finally ready to do this?"

"Yes." Her eyes sparkled with mischief. "Did you bring the Benz? Mom volunteered to stay home."

"No such luck. I borrowed a car again."

Fitting, Courtney thought, since she was sort of a borrowed "date." And so was Gabe.

"All set?" Gabe looked at Ava, then her. When they both nodded, he said, "Let's go."

Courtney was happy to have her daughter along and avoid awkward silences on the drive. No time to think about that hot kiss and what had almost happened. Ava was in a good mood, excited to see the animals. What with being a single mom, Courtney was aware that her daughter had had to grow up faster than kids who had two parents. It was great to see her acting like a kid.

After parking, they walked to the entrance, where Gabe bought admission tickets and was given a map of the zoo and the botanical gardens along with a brochure about the attractions.

He glanced through it. "If we hurry, we can make the giraffe feeding. It only happens at certain times."

"Oh my God!" Ava's eyes went wide. "Mom, can we go?"

"Yes." She looked up at Gabe. "Okay?"

"It would take a stronger man than me to say no to those faces. But there's no time to waste, ladies. It starts in a few minutes. We have to hustle." He checked the map, then pointed. "That way."

They headed in the right direction, and Ava set a swift pace, nearly running. Courtney and Gabe walked side by side a little behind her. When their hands brushed, she felt it all the way to her toes, and that was before he spontaneously linked his fingers with hers. It seemed natural, but of course it was just for show. Somehow she needed to get that message to the parts of her that were squealing with delight.

Ava arrived at the giraffe enclosure just a little before them. "Hurry, it's about to start. There's a five-dollar fee, but you get to feed them."

Courtney started to pull out her wallet, but Gabe was already handing the park attendant some bills. Inside, one of the animal care workers gave out branches of acacia leaves. Gabe pushed his into Ava's hands, and she smiled up at him. The animals were separated from them by a sturdy metal fence, and when the teen held out the leaves, a big, graceful head leaned over the top and munched on them.

"Mom, look at me!"

"I see, sweetie. I'll get a picture." She pulled out her cell phone and swiped the screen for the camera. After centering Ava and the adorable long-lashed, long-necked creature, she tapped the white button. "Got it."

"I'll get one of you with her," Gabe offered.

"Thanks." How thoughtful was that? She handed the phone to him and walked over to her daughter. They stood on either side of the giraffe, and he got the photo.

It was crowded, and people were waiting their turn with the charming and charismatic animals. They moved out of the way and went to stand beside Gabe.

Thirty minutes in giraffe heaven had Ava beaming up at him, hero worship shining in her eyes. "Thank you for bringing me today."

"You're welcome. But we have a lot more zoo to get through," he said.

"If I don't see another thing, I still had a great time. That was completely awesome."

"It really was," Courtney told him.

"Why don't I get a picture of you guys by the giraffes," Ava offered.

"That's all right," Courtney said. "We do have a lot more to look at—"

"That's a great idea, Ava." Gabe slid her a challenging look.

"Just do it, Mom."

"Okay." She handed over the phone.

Gabe put his hand to the small of her back and guided her to the metal enclosure. Everywhere his fingers touched set her on fire and made her want to lean into him. All she could think about was sex.

Ava held up the camera. "Got it. One more."

With an all clear, Courtney moved away quickly, as if she'd been burned. Which she had. They stayed with the giraffes until the animal care workers closed down the enclosure. Ava was disappointed there wasn't more time.

"There's still lots of stuff to see." Gabe was trying to make it better. "What do you want to do now?"

"Can we go to the petting zoo?" the teen asked.

"Of course."

He referred to the map, pointed them in the right direction and off they went. It wasn't too far, and when Ava saw the baby goats and sheep, she squealed with excitement. She hurried ahead of them and went through the gate into the pen to give the enthusiastic animals some love. When she found the brushes for untangling an animal's matted hair Courtney sighed.

She looked up at Gabe. "We're going to be here for a while."

"I kind of figured that, judging by her reaction."

"You don't mind?"

"Absolutely not. She obviously loves animals and is having a good time." He leaned against the low fence, settling in for the duration. "We're in no hurry. No schedule today," he assured her.

Courtney watched the sheep and goats crowd in around her daughter as she brushed one of the babies. "She wants a dog, but with both of us gone so much, I don't think it's fair to an animal. Maybe a cat, though."

"Can I ask you a question?"

She met his gaze but couldn't see what he was thinking with his eyes covered by the dark, sexy aviator sunglasses. "Yes. But I reserve the right not to answer."

"This is an easy one, I think." He smiled. "Did something happen between you and Ava before I picked you up?"

"Why do you ask?"

"I'm not sure. You seemed a little subdued, I guess."

Wasn't he the observant one. There was no reason not to tell him. "I had second thoughts about her coming today. Not because of you, exactly." She shrugged. "I just don't want her getting too attached.

She's been hurt before because of choices I made and she was stuck with."

"The ex-husband?"

"Yeah." *Creep.* "I met Adam at the hospital. He's a sales rep for an equipment company. We clicked fast, and he wanted to get married and have a family. He understood that Ava and I were a package deal and said all the right things. He loved her and wanted to be a father to her. And I fell for that line."

"How do you know it was a line?"

"Because after we were married, he wanted a baby right away. He said he wanted 'real' kids. When I pointed out Ava *is* a real kid, he said he wanted one that had his blood. And that's a quote."

A muscle in his jaw moved as his mouth pulled tight for a moment. "Jerk."

"I called him worse." She looked away for a moment. "Even after I knew he lied, I tried to make it work, because it was one more mistake on my record. But I couldn't agree to a baby right away. What he'd said didn't sit right with me and doubts crept in. The truth is, because of how badly I wanted a family for her, I stayed much too long. I won't make that mistake again. I realized that Ava and I are a family. We don't need anyone else to complete us."

"I get it."

"I just don't want her caught in the middle of something a second time. This thing with you and me is supposed to protect everyone we love. But I saw how excited she was this morning to see you and come here."

"I understand," he said quietly. "I just thought including her would be a good thing. From now on, I won't. I'm not him, Courtney. And she's a terrific kid. I would never deliberately do anything to hurt her."

"I know." She was close enough that his legs brushed against hers, and sparks flew. But she didn't move away. "And another thing. Apparently she knows me better than I realized."

"Why do you say that?"

"I was trying to warn her not to get attached. She actually said I have a bad attitude about dating. Then she accused me of having an exit strategy with you. That I was already convinced things wouldn't work out."

"Did she?" He grinned, and it was full of wickedness.

"This isn't funny," she protested, although a smile tugged at her mouth. "I guess I was a little too adamant about her not getting attached to you, about you and me not being more than friends. In case things with us go south. In a nasty way."

"And they will. Although it won't be nasty," he added. "We have our insurance policy in place to prevent that exact scenario."

"Right," she agreed. "But she met you. She likes you, and now we're walking a fine line. I don't want her to get hurt when we end things. But for this to work, she has to believe that I cared deeply and need time to get over you."

"I know. So here's to keeping up appearances."

He took her hand and tugged her between his knees, then kissed her lightly on the mouth.

Courtney's heart hammered. Her hands and feet tingled. Liquid heat poured through her. She smiled and said, "Kissing class paid off. No bumps, bruises or concussions that time."

"I am a tutor, after all."

But this had nothing to do with math. It was chemistry, and she was feeling the reaction. That kiss complicated the heck out of this crazy agreement. Because sex was sounding better and better, especially now that she was on the pill. This wasn't part of their deal, but what was wrong with having sex? They were friends and liked each other. If her response to his kiss was any indication, there was a mutual attraction.

It wasn't love. Period. She had physical and emotional protections in place and could proceed wherever her hormones led her. Okay, she thought, now that her head was on straight, she could look forward to whatever was next.

On Monday at work, Gabe filled in for Carla, who was sick. He answered phones, talked to walk-in clients, and a couple of them even signed a short-term contract for matchmaking services. The morning flew by, and suddenly it was afternoon. He didn't realize how much time had passed until sandwiches that his aunt had ordered for lunch were delivered. Lil came out of her office to announce it was time to eat and instructed him to lock the door, then turn calls over to the answering service.

She carried the bag of food to the break room and set it on the small table before sitting down. "Will you get us some drinks from the fridge, dear? A bottled water is fine for me."

He grabbed two and sat at a right angle to her, where his sandwich was waiting. "Suddenly I'm starved."

"Mondays are always busy." She took a bite of her food and chewed delicately.

"I had no idea."

"Because you hibernate in your office. Carla could have told you." She wiped her mouth with a napkin, then smiled. "How much more do you appreciate her now?"

"So much more," he said with feeling. For several moments, they ate in silence. Then Gabe thought about what she'd said. "So Mondays are always this busy?"

"Most hectic day of the week," she confirmed. "That's why Carla felt so bad about not coming in to work. But she sounded just terrible. Hacking and coughing. Could hardly talk, poor thing. Not good when a large portion of your responsibility is dealing with phone calls."

"True."

"Plus, whatever she has needs to be quarantined." She shuddered. "I don't want to get it."

"Me, either."

He didn't want to be contagious when he kissed

Courtney again. There was no point in promising himself it wasn't going to happen. She was like popcorn at a movie theater. You could swear up and down you weren't eating any, but when it was right in front of you, good intentions went out the window and you ordered an extra large. He felt that way every time he looked at her mouth, every time she smiled and flashed those dynamite dimples.

"You're looking thoughtful about something." His aunt's expression was both curious and knowing.

Gabe didn't want to go there with her again. "Tell me why Monday is so reliably the busiest day of the week?"

"It's the first business day after the weekend." She said that as if it was obvious, but he must have looked completely clueless because she continued. "Two days can feel like two weeks if you're lonely and have no one to share them with. And sometimes we get a call because they've shared it with the wrong person. Or broken up painfully. Or found out their best someone is cheating. Being proactive is a very good way to handle heartbreak." The look on her face said that last one was specifically directed at him.

"All of that makes perfect sense." And he was officially sorry he'd asked. "What did you do this weekend?"

"Not much." She smiled as if he'd gone right where she wanted him to go. "But yours was good."

It wasn't a question. "How do you know?"

"You look happier than I've seen you for a very long time."

"I don't look any different."

"Anyone who knows you can see it," she protested.

"No," he said. "For better or worse, I'm the same me."

"Oh please. I'm old, not deaf, dumb and blind. You haven't snapped at anyone all morning. In fact, all day you've been nothing but gracious. Charming, even. Did it escape your notice that all the new clients you signed up today were women?"

"Really? I'm always pleasant. Dare I add charismatic?" He grinned, and she returned it.

"Maybe I should put you out front more often. I'll give you polite, maybe. But not generally charming. There's a difference today for some reason," she assured him. "I've gotten so used to grumpy Gabe that this new upbeat attitude is freaking me out a little."

"I'm not that bad." He took a bite of sandwich and washed it down with water.

"I hate to break it to you, but you really can be that bad. And generally you are." She reached over and patted his arm. "But not today. Why is that, I wonder?"

"No idea. But I don't think I'm any different. I think you're imagining things."

"I do have a vivid imagination," she allowed. "But that's not what this is. Don't forget how well I know you, Gabriel. Since you were born, as a matter of fact."

"I know you, too. And you see things as you want

them to be." He held up a hand. "Don't get me wrong. I love that about you."

She smiled fondly. "And I you. Don't tell your siblings this, because I absolutely adore all of you. But you're the son I never had. My favorite."

"And you're mine."

"Dear boy." She smiled. "I'm telling you that because it means that I notice everything. And this happy Gabe tells me that whatever issue you had with Courtney has been satisfactorily resolved."

Good guess, he thought, remembering that phone conversation. The one where she admitted to still being in recovery from the intensity of the kiss. And said she needed to be on birth control. He went hot just thinking about it.

"We did talk," he admitted.

"And?"

"I took her and Ava to the zoo on Saturday."

"So things with her are going well. That makes me very happy, because I've been awfully worried about you." She nodded her approval, but there were tears in her eyes.

And there was visual confirmation that the plan was working. That realization was followed closely by guilt. She was happy because of something that wasn't real. When did guilt become his BFF? And who knew there were so many kinds?

Guilt that he'd lived and Margo didn't. Shame for the first time he'd laughed out loud after she died, as if his life without her hadn't turned upside down and inside out. Remorse for all the firsts he'd experienced without her. And now, the very special guilt for deceiving his aunt who was like a second mother to him. There was a place in hell with his name burned into it.

"Don't go popping the champagne cork just yet. I'm not the only one who's had a hard time. Courtney is dealing with a lot of baggage, too."

Teenage pregnancy and abandonment by the baby's father. Somehow the jackass she married was even worse. Gabe wasn't a scared high school kid. He wasn't the man who'd led Courtney to believe something that wasn't true in order to get what he wanted.

Although he saw the parallels between that and his current situation with her, he refused to believe it was the same thing. Courtney had signed off on their plan with all the necessary information and her eyes wide-open. She was doing it in order to avoid a third mistake. Proactive, as his aunt would say.

"Look, Aunt Lil, just cool your jets on this. We're taking things slow."

"There's slow," she said thoughtfully, "and then there's stuck in neutral. You were there even before meeting Courtney. And you've been in that place way too long, Gabriel."

He couldn't argue with that. Unbeknownst to her, he was actually still idling in neutral. "We're just getting to know each other."

"This will probably get me in trouble, but I'm going to say it anyway." She met his gaze. "Have you kissed her? And I mean a good one. Not like that one on the patio at your mother's house. And no, I didn't see it, but I've heard a lot about your performance."

"Yes, I've kissed her again." And it had been pretty awesome, if he did say so himself.

"Thank goodness," she said. "But time is wasting. You need to sleep with Courtney."

He should have been prepared for that. This woman was known for saying outrageous things. "Aunt Lil!"

"Sex has been around for a long time," she huffed. "Not talking about it won't change that. And I'll say it again. You need to have sex with her before she comes to the conclusion that there's something wrong with you."

Well, he thought. He would see her outrageous and raise her some. "How do you know I haven't already slept with her?"

She laughed, then got that mysterious look she was famous for. "I just know."

"I will neither confirm nor deny." He took a really big bite of his sandwich, because it gave him an excuse not to talk with his mouth full.

He was definitely not going to confirm to his aunt that he planned to have sex with Courtney at their earliest possible convenience.

Chapter Ten

It was Friday night, almost a week since the zoo trip, and Courtney was waiting for Gabe to come over. Again she was nervous, but not about her clothes or meeting his family. This time she was fixing dinner, and Ava was going to a sleepover at a friend's house. She would be alone with him.

After work she had put on jeans and a T-shirt, very casual. She freshened her makeup, dragged a brush through her hair and left it free to fall past her shoulders. The last step was a neutral lip gloss. She looked presentable, not provocative. There were no expectations, but that didn't mean no anticipation. Excitement was humming through her in spite of every effort to squash it.

She blew out a cleansing breath, turned off the

bedroom light and walked out the door and into the hall. Ava was in her room putting together her things for the overnighter.

"Don't forget your toothbrush." Courtney rested a shoulder against the doorjamb.

"Got it." Ava held up two sweaters—one left her midriff bare, and the other was blue with a scalloped hem that came well down over her waist. "Which one should I wear tomorrow?"

"I like the blue on you."

"Because it covers all the skin." Ava wasn't asking.

"I'm not gonna lie." Courtney shrugged. "What are you girls going to do tonight?"

"Probably order pizza and watch movies."

"So you're staying in?"

Ava rolled her eyes. "We're not meeting boys, if that's what you're asking."

"It's like you can read my mind," Courtney teased.

She knew her daughter was beautiful and boys had to be noticing. As far as she could tell, Ava always socialized with a group of kids and didn't pair off, but that would change. The two of them had agreed that she wouldn't date one on one until she was sixteen, and she would come to her if she needed the pill. There was only so much a mother could control. Courtney just had to hope that Ava would always be open and honest about her activities.

When the thought went through her mind, she winced. *She* was the one not telling the truth, although she was doing her best to be as honest as possible. Everything was true except that both she and Gabe knew their time together had an expiration date, which was yet to be determined.

Ava tossed the too-short sweater on the bed and put the other one in the duffel bag with sweatpants and a T-shirt to sleep in. "I promise it's just a few girls. Boys are so immature and gross."

"That's the spirit."

Ava sighed. "You're so weird."

"Thank you." She glanced around the chaos of the room. "If you forgot anything, just text. I'll try to locate it in here and run it over to you."

"I'm not five. I don't need my blankie anymore."

"Am I a horrible mother for saying I liked it better when you were this many?" She held up her hand with five fingers splayed.

Ava slung the straps of the duffel over her arm and headed out the door. Her voice drifted back as she descended the stairs. "This is why you need a steady boyfriend."

Courtney followed. "Even if I had a boyfriend, I would still get mushy about when you were a little girl."

"But if you had a boyfriend, and please let Mr. B be the one, I wouldn't have to feel bad when you get all freaked out about me growing up."

She made a mental note to edit the mush and not let this child see how much the growing up too fast was killing her. She just loved this kid to the moon and back and wanted her to always know. Was that really so bad?

Ava dropped her bag by the front door. "When is Mr. B getting here anyway?"

"Soon."

"What are you making him for dinner?"

"Chicken with mushroom sauce over rice. Salad. Fruit for dessert. I made everything last night and just have to reheat."

"Yum. It's good. He'll like that. It's one of my favorites."

"I made plenty," Courtney said. "You could stay home. Skip girls' night." Then she kicked herself for not editing the mush. "Kidding, kiddo. Who's picking you up?"

"Lexi and her mom are coming by since I'm right on the way to Becca's. She'll text when they get here."

"Okay."

There was a knock on the door, and Courtney jumped. She'd been distracted, but that didn't stop Gabe nerves from being on high alert.

"I'll get it." Ava was standing at the bottom of the stairs, steps from the door. She turned the knob, pulled it open, and there he stood with a bouquet of flowers and a bottle of wine. "Hey, Mr. B. Come on in."

"Thanks. Is your mom—" He walked in and saw her standing there. "Oh, hi. You look pretty."

"You don't have to say that just because we're—"

"Mom," Ava said, "just accept a compliment gracefully."

"That's what I always tell you," she acknowledged. But he wasn't really a candidate for boyfriend and shouldn't feel obligated to tell her she looked nice. The words had almost slipped out and would have blown their cover. Instead she said, "Thanks, Gabe. You look nice, too."

"Oh, this old thing?" He looked down at his jeans, pullover sweater and brown leather jacket.

Courtney laughed. Leave it to him to lighten the moment. "And flowers, too, just like a real—"

"Lexi's here." Ava apparently hadn't heard the second near slip. "I gotta go. 'Bye, Mom. See ya, Mr. B."

"Have fun," Courtney called out just before the door slammed shut. She stared at it for several moments, then looked at Gabe. "Welcome to freak-out central. Ava just told me she feels bad when I get all weird about her going out with friends. And that's why I need a boyfriend."

"Hmm." His eyebrows rose, and he held up the bottle of white in his hand. "Sounds like a story there. Should we have wine?"

His words snapped her out of it. "Yes. Sorry. I've got an electric opener in the kitchen. And the flowers really are beautiful."

"Just like a real date," he said wryly. "That's what you were going to say, right?"

"Saved by the bell. Or text," she clarified. "Ava would have picked right up on that. And, seriously, the flowers are a very nice touch."

"Not for show, actually. I picked up the wine, saw the sunflowers and thought of you. An impulse buy."

Be still my heart. But it didn't listen and continued to pound away. "That's very sweet. I don't quite know what to make of you."

"Why?" He found the opener charging on the kitchen counter and took the cork out of the bottle.

"You really throw yourself into a role," she said. "With props and everything."

"I'm an exemplary dinner guest."

And so much more. She pulled two glasses from the cupboard beside him then pointed to the top shelf. "Would you mind getting that for me?"

"Of course." He grabbed the vase easily and lifted it down.

"Thanks." At the sink she filled it with water. The sunflowers and greens fit perfectly. "So pretty and cheerful."

"Just like you."

"Ava's gone. You don't have to stay in character and keep up the act."

"I'm being completely sincere." He took off his jacket and settled it over the back of a kitchen chair. "You *are* beautiful and cheerful."

That did it. Her heart was incapable of being still. Her breath caught when she recognized the intensity in his eyes. Had they always been such a vivid blue, or was something else going on right here and now? Just for her. Nervous tension kicked in again with enthusiasm.

"Are you hungry? I'm starved." She moved in front of the refrigerator, preparing to open it. "It's all cooked. I just have to reheat everything. Except salad. But it's not leftovers, I promise. Just cooked everything ahead of time. The table is set. All I have to do is put dressing on the greens and—"

Gabe put a finger to her lips to stop the verbal diarrhea. "You're jumpy."

"No way. I'm just—" His grin put the brakes on her denial. "Okay, yes. I figured kissing class would be in session again soon. During dinner, I planned to tell you that I'm on the pill. There, that wasn't awkward at all. Did you notice how I slipped that information organically into the conversation?"

"I did. But I am out of practice interpreting a woman's intentions. Let's clarify." He wasn't grinning now, but searching her face intently. "Are you saying that you want to have sex?"

"When we discussed our rules of engagement, the conversation never included what to do or not do about it. We only talked about neither of us looking for love."

Gabe moved to stand in front of her. He looked down, and his voice was a tender and warm whisper when he said, "This won't change that."

"I should hope not." She smiled. "So I'm saying yes. The kissing curriculum can include sex."

"Okay. School is officially in session." Gabe settled his palms on the refrigerator, on either side of her, then leaned in and kissed her.

Courtney was lost the moment his lips touched hers. She put her arms around his neck and nestled her body as close to his as she could get. He slid his fingers into her hair and cupped the back of her head, making the contact of their mouths more firm.

He touched his tongue to her top lip. When she opened to him, he dipped inside, the move every bit as raw and unapologetic as it was seductive. The refrigerator was right there behind her, and he moved her back into it, knocking off a magnet holding papers. Neither of them paid any attention.

He pressed against her, and it was as if he kissed her with his entire body. The movement ignited a fire that spread to her blood, and liquid warmth poured through her. She could tell he was feeling it, too, the way his lips frantically moved across her cheek, her eyelids, her chin, then nuzzled her ear and nipped her neck. She could feel his heart pounding, and satisfaction spilled through her at the same time she wondered how much more of this could she take.

She was breathing so hard it was possible she wouldn't be able to get the words out but gave it a try. "G-Gabe?"

"Hmm?"

His mouth was on her neck, and the single response vibrated through her, making her moan. "I was wondering—"

"Yes?"

"I just thought—" The stroke of his tongue near her ear made her gasp.

"What are you wondering?" he whispered. He slid his hand under her T-shirt, up over her ribs, and brushed the underside of her breast with his thumb.

"Oh, sweet mother of mercy—"

There was a smile in his voice when he said, "What were you saying?"

"I forgot." She couldn't think. His fingers were doing things, and her world was narrowed to nothing but his touch.

When his hand closed over her breast, sensations raced through her with a force that left her weak in the knees. And she remembered what she'd been about to say.

"I was wondering if you would like to see what the upstairs of my place looks like. Particularly my bedroom."

"I would like that very much." His smile was tender, just before he dropped a featherlight kiss on her mouth and took her hand. "Lead the way."

Without a word, they walked up the stairs and into her feminine sanctuary, with its queen-size floral comforter and pink-and-plum-colored throw pillows. Some of them even had sequins. Light filtered in from the hall, and she smiled at the contrast of his intense masculinity here in her girlie space.

With his help, Courtney turned down the covers, and from either side of the bed they stared intently at each other. She could see the rapid rise and fall of his chest, and that had her own breathing stuttering wildly.

A moment later, he moved around the foot of the bed, stopping inches from her. There was a smoky, hungry look in his eyes that torched through her like fire licking her insides. The next moment they were kissing, tugging at each other's clothes. When jeans, shirts, sweater and everything else were tossed wherever, they came together on the mattress.

The feel of his hands on her naked skin was like tossing kerosene on a fire. When he touched her breast, heat shot straight down to her belly, and lower.

He ran his palm down the inside of her thigh, then gently parted her legs and knelt between them. She reached out for him, and he came to her, taking his weight on his forearms. A tiny moan of anticipation caught in her throat as she wrapped her legs around his waist and urged him toward her.

Slowly he entered her, and she sighed with satisfaction as he began to move. Her breathing escalated, and it felt as if she couldn't get enough air into her lungs. With three hard thrusts of his hips, he had pleasure splintering inside her. He held her close as aftershocks of her release trembled through her and finally stopped.

Then he began to move again, and she arched her hips, accepting him as he sank into her over and over. His breathing grew more labored and harsher until he groaned and went still, gathering her close. She held him tight as the spasms of his own pleasure slowed and finally stopped.

He sighed into her hair. "Just so you know... I really like your bedroom."

She smiled. "It's the highlight of the tour."

After they quickly cleaned up, Gabe settled her beside him as if reluctant to let her go. *He's an after-sex snuggler*, she thought sleepily. Being nervous must have sapped her energy, because she dozed off in his arms for a while. When she woke, the lighted clock on the nightstand indicated a couple of hours had passed. And she was starving, because they'd never had dinner.

"Gabe?" she whispered.

"Hmm?" His voice was sleepy.

"It's late-ish."

He turned his head to look at the clock, then rubbed a hand over his face. "Wow. Sorry. I fell asleep."

"Me, too. Are you hungry?"

"Starved."

She raised up on an elbow. "I never fed you. Obviously that makes me the world's worst hostess."

He took the strand of hair falling over her face and tucked it behind her ear. "I think you are the consummate hostess."

"Very funny." Her tone was sarcastic, but she couldn't stop a grin at his pun. "I'm going to warm everything up."

"I'm already warm."

She laughed. "I meant food."

"Count me in," he said.

They dressed quickly and went down to the kitchen, where it took all of five minutes to toss salad and heat dinner. Their wine was warm, but they drank it anyway.

Gabe tasted the chicken, and his eyes widened. "This is really good."

"Ava said you'd like it." And suddenly she lost her appetite as the situation hit her. What could have happened. She got up and found her phone on the countertop beside the stove, then checked for messages. Fortunately, there weren't any.

"What's bothering you?"

"Why would you think something's wrong?"

"I know you." Fork in hand, he met her gaze. "And the way you shot out of your chair after mentioning Ava."

She met his gaze. "Ava could have walked in on us."

"But she's gone for the night."

"She was gone less than ten minutes before we were upstairs. What if she forgot something and came home for it? I left my phone down here, and she could have messaged that she would come by." She pushed the food around her plate. "I've had conversations with her about sex. Protection. But I've also told her that she should be in love before taking the step."

"In a perfect world, that would be the case, but more often than not, sex follows when hormones are out of control." His tone was patient and reasonable.

"I know. But she's a romantic, and I want her first time to be special." *Like tonight was for me.* Later she would think about the significance of that impulsive thought. "But if she walked in on us, that makes me a do as I say, not as I do kind of mom."

"Okay. Message received."

"Thank you for understanding my need to be careful with her."

"Of course."

Courtney would be careful in another way, too. Her first time with Gabe had felt special, but that didn't mean she was going to the next level with him. Sex didn't change what they were, what this was—a practical solution to their mutual problem. If they had some fun along the way, what could it hurt?

It was Tuesday, and Gabe was at the high school for his tutoring day. He was using Brett's classroom while his friend had a math department staff meeting. A few students had come in to ask questions about their homework and left after doing one or two equations and feeling confident about the material. They seemed to grasp the concept and were just making sure their calculations were right.

Now he was alone and bored, so he pulled out his cell phone to check for messages. Hoping to see something from Courtney. But nada. That was a letdown, and he wondered why. Per their rules of engagement, there should be no expectations. And yet...

Maybe the discontent had something to do with what a fantastic time he'd had at her place. And not just the sex, which was pretty great. But dinner was delicious, albeit a little on the late side. That made him smile because of *why* it had been so late. Mostly the evening had just been fun. Courtney was fun, and that body...

There were voices in the hall just before two kids walked into the classroom. The boy was in baggy jeans and a black T-shirt and badly needed a haircut. The other kid was Ava. She was smiling at the scruffy boy, and it was not the look of a girl who didn't like her companion. That wasn't good, along with the fact that he'd just been thinking about sleeping with her mother. Somehow, protecting Ava from the fallout of that seemed less urgent than this boy she was laughing with.

"Hi, Mr. B. This is my friend Nick Perino."

"Hey, Nick." Gabe put his hand out, and the kid took it with a firm grip. That earned him a few points. "You guys need math help?"

"I'm not sure he does." Ava glanced at her friend. "But, yeah, I'm a little lost."

"Okay. Let's see what we're looking at."

The teens sat side by side at a desk, and Ava opened her book. Gabe looked over the lesson on solving two-step algebra equations. "Okay. Obviously your teacher went over this. Let's do your homework, and we'll go through each equation step by step and make sure you understand it."

After pulling out notebooks and pencils from their backpacks, they wrote down the first equation. Ava looked like she wanted to throw the book across the room. "I don't even know where to start."

"That's what I'm here for," he reassured her. "The first step is to visualize a solution. You're solving for x, and you have to decide whether to use addition or subtraction to isolate the variable."

Ava looked at her paper, then at him. "Still not clicking."

He pointed out the numbers she'd written. "Find

a way to keep the whole numbers on one side of the equal sign. Remember, whatever you do to one side has to be done to the other. Keep it balanced."

"Yeah," Nick said. "Our teacher keeps repeating that. It's the golden rule of algebra, she says."

"She's right. So give it a try." Gabe watched them work and nodded. "Now you have to add the whole numbers on both sides."

He noticed that Nick was already finished, then nodded when Ava stopped writing. "Good job. Now try the next one."

They wrote it down, and he observed them, noting the answer was right. Nick was faster than Ava, and he had a feeling Ava was right about this kid not really needing help. He was only here to spend time with her. Bad boys were to teenage girls what metal was to a magnet.

That did not make him happy and gave his protective instincts a kick in the ass. What would he do if she was his daughter? The answer was instant and not the least bit rational. He'd send her to a convent school.

As Ava wrote down each step of the next equation, he nodded approval or pointed out where she was going wrong. Nick was doing just fine on his own and working ahead, which made Gabe's distrust even more acute. And, wow, that made absolutely no sense at all.

Ava finished up the last equation without needing any help and smiled at him. "Is that right?"

"It is," he confirmed. "Good job."

As the kids were packing up their stuff, his friend Brett walked into the room. "Hey, guys."

"Hi, Mr. Kamp." Ava smiled. "I'm here to improve my math grade. Don't you think I should get extra credit for making the effort?"

"That's up to your teacher. But nice try." He grinned then looked at her friend. "How are you doing, Nick?"

The kid slid down lower in the chair and crossed his arms over his chest. "Just hanging out."

Ava looked at him then stood. "We have to go. Thanks for the help, Mr. B."

"So, you think you've got it now?" he asked.

"Maybe." She shrugged. "I'm going to give my brain a rest now."

Gabe laughed. "Good idea."

"See you later." Ava walked out of the room and mumbled something to Nick.

Gabe wanted to know what. And after that he really wanted to warn Nick that if he hurt that girl, there would be hell to pay. As soon as that thought crossed his mind, the irony, not to mention the hypocrisy, smacked him upside the head. He was fake dating her mother. That could potentially hurt Ava. So who was going to give him hell?

"Just have to make sure she never finds out," he muttered.

Brett was walking over to his desk and set his laptop case down. "What was that?"

"Nothing." Gabe turned to look at him. "What do you know about that kid?"

"Ava?"

"No. The boy."

"Ah." Brett leaned back against his desk and crossed one ankle over the other. "He's smart. I mean high-IQ intelligent. His grades are okay, but he could be an honors student. He's not performing to his potential."

"So you're saying Ava should not hang out with him?"

"I didn't say that." His friend gave him an odd look. "He's more of a rebel. Likes to push the envelope, you know? But not in any trouble that I'm aware of. I don't think he's a bad kid."

"But he could be?" Gabe was looking for an informed opinion.

"It's a good sign that he was here for tutoring with Ava."

"He doesn't need it."

"I know," Brett said. "But he cares enough about her to come along. Just to spend time with her. And you want to know this, why?"

Gabe looked down for a moment, then met his friend's gaze. "I'm going out with her mother."

Brett grinned with enthusiastic approval. "That's really great."

"It's not a big deal. We met here at the freshman motivational talk." No reason for him to reveal Ava's part in pushing them together.

"But you're clearly not an impartial observer. You're feeling protective. Is it some kind of sign that you're getting serious about her mom?"

Not a chance. He and Courtney had taken care of that.

"We're just friends. Taking it slow. She's got baggage and so do I. As you know."

"Yeah. But the fact that you're dating is a step up for you."

"It's not romantic. Just getting to know each other." *Naked*, he thought and smiled inside.

"Isn't that what everyone says just before taking a plunge into the relationship pool?"

Gabe couldn't help grinning. "It's a good thing you're a math teacher instead of creative writing. That was groan worthy."

"Maybe." Brett shrugged. "But look at you just now. Ready to warn Nick that if he steps out of line with Ava, no more tutoring for him."

"Some warning. That kid could tutor Ava." He took that one step further in his mind and figured not much math would get done. "Scratch that."

"See?"

That made Gabe smile and shake his head. "You have quite the romantic streak. I had no idea. If you ever think about switching careers, you could go to work for my aunt at Make Me a Match."

"No way. Math is dependable."

"Okay. But depend on this—Courtney and I are nothing more than friends. We're having fun. And I'm just treating Ava like any other kid."

"I don't believe you." The other man sighed. "Now, don't bite my head off for this, but someday

when you have kids, you're going to be a great father."

Gabe could have had kids, but fate had robbed
him of that chance when Margo died.

Brett straightened away from the desk. "Okay,
my friend, I would love to continue this discussion,
but I have a meeting with the principal. That means
I need to lock up the classroom."

"Okay."

Gabe walked with his friend as far as the ad-
ministration building, then continued out to the fac-
ulty parking lot. He unlocked the Benz and got in
but didn't start the engine. His friend's words ran
through his mind. *You're going to be a great father.*

Normally a comment like that would trigger his
anger response, but not this time. He felt exposed
without it, like he was going into battle without tac-
tical gear, and he didn't much like the feeling.

What he did like was Brett's reaction to Gabe
dating Courtney. His friend was buying the reality
of them as a couple, exactly what he and Courtney
were going for.

But he'd expected to achieve this result with his
emotional shields in place, and it made him uncomfortable to realize his defenses were down. It was
a good news/bad news scenario that confused the
hell out of him.

Chapter Eleven

If anyone had told Courtney that she would call off dinner plans with a handsome man who was a god in bed, she'd have recommended admitting that person to the hospital psych ward. But that's what she was going to do. It had been a brutal day on every level, and she wouldn't be good company. They'd agreed this fake fling would be about having fun, but a "date" tonight would make a lie of that promise.

After walking in the door from work, she called out, "Ava, I'm home."

"Upstairs, Mom," came the faint, music-to-her-ears reply.

It was what her kid always said, but after her terrible, very bad, sad day, those words and her daughter's voice were even more precious. Courtney was physically and emotionally drained, and making the trip upstairs was almost more than she could manage. But manage it she did.

At the top she hung her purse on the post, then went into Ava's room. Her child was sprawled on the bed, surrounded by books and papers.

"Hi, Mom." She smiled and sat up on the edge of the bed.

Courtney couldn't get to her fast enough, and when she did, pulling Ava into her arms didn't feel soon enough. "Hi, baby."

"Are you okay?" There was concern in Ava's voice.

"I am now." She breathed in the familiar flowery fragrance of shampoo and let out a sigh of relief that her child's body was warm. That she was still breathing. "I just needed to see you. Bad day at work."

Ava leaned back and studied her. "You look tired."

"I'm way beyond that."

"Aren't you going out with Mr. B tonight?"

"We were supposed to, but I'm going to cancel."

"Maybe you should take a shower before you do that. It might perk you up. I thought you were looking forward to seeing him."

"I was." That was more true than she wanted it to be. Thoughts of an evening with Gabe had gotten her through some rough moments today. They'd been going out for nearly two months now, and that included a lot of Sunday dinners with his family. If anything, her anticipation of spending time with him showed no sign of fading. "It's better if I cancel. I'm doing him a favor, believe me. Although a hot shower sounds like heaven."

"Then that's what you should do."

Courtney didn't want to stop looking at her girl. She memorized every curve of that sweet, innocent face, every single freckle, and promised to be grateful she was on this earth, even when pushed to the limits of her patience.

"Okay, sweetie. I'm going to call Gabe, then take a long, hot shower." She kissed Ava's cheek and smiled. "I love you to the moon and back."

"I love you more."

She hugged her teen one more time, then left before Ava could be weirded out. After grabbing her purse, she pulled out her cell phone and headed to her own room. With a tired sigh, she sat on the bed, the same one where he'd made her body remember how life-affirming sex was. She sighed, hit speed dial, then listened to the ring. He answered before a second one sounded.

"Hi," he said. "I'm just about ready to head over and pick you up. There's a new Italian restaurant I'd like to try if you're game—"

"About that, could I get a rain check?"

"Of course." But he hesitated. "Is something wrong? Are you okay? Ava?"

"She's fine. I'm just—it was a really bad day at work and—" Suddenly there was a lump in her throat the size of a Toyota. She was afraid sobs would start and she wouldn't be able to stop.

"Court?"

She took a calming breath. "Sorry. I'm putting myself in quarantine. I don't want this mood to bring you down, too."

"Maybe I could cheer you up. And a nice dinner out might just be what you need to—"

"That's sweet, but I'm exhausted."

"You have to eat." There was genuine concern in his tone.

"I'm not very hungry. I'll just throw something together for Ava."

"Good. She's there with you."

"Yes." Thank God. Tonight another mother and father weren't so lucky. "I'm fine, Gabe, really. Let's talk in a couple of days. In fact, this cancellation can work in our favor. Pretty soon we have to start showing 'tension in the relationship' to make our 'breakup' believable." Nearly half of that statement was in air quotes. Tonight she didn't have the emotional reserves to not be oddly irritated by that. "We'll talk soon. And strategize."

"Yeah," he said. "Talk soon."

Courtney said goodbye and clicked off. Then she stripped out of her hospital scrubs, bra and panties, and threw them into the hamper with a force that surprised her. The crappy day wasn't their fault.

In the bathroom she turned on the shower as hot as she could stand it and just stood under the water. It relaxed her even though there was no way this could wash away the memory of that dead teenager's face. But she needed to feel clean and massaged shampoo into her hair, then soaped her body and rinsed away what she could. This would have to be enough.

She toweled off, put on sweatpants and a ratty, long-sleeved T-shirt, then blow-dried her hair and pulled it into a ponytail. After patting moisturizer on her face, she did feel a little better and had the stirrings of an appetite.

Heading toward the stairs, she poked her head into Ava's room. "You hungry?"

"I ate before you got home from work," she said.

"You still have homework?"

"Yeah." She put on her most pathetic face. "Have I mentioned recently how much I hate school?"

"I believe I have a text on my phone from this morning addressing that very thing. Sorry, I can't help you out there." And thank goodness it wasn't life or death.

"Go eat, Mom."

"Okay."

She went downstairs to the kitchen and opened the refrigerator, which was bizarrely empty. "Note to self—go grocery shopping."

Maybe the freezer had something. She seemed to remember a frozen dinner. It was gone, so she figured that's what Ava had. No miracles for her today. Until she spotted ice cream.

"Why not?" She grabbed the container and a spoon and had the lid removed before reaching the kitchen table.

Just as she was ready to dig in, there was a knock on the door. Maybe Ava had texted one of her friends for something to do with homework. Probably math answers. She peeked through the window and saw Gabe standing there. Her first reaction was completely physical—heart pounding, pulse racing and a spike in her breathing. Her second response was totally female. She looked like crap.

A second knock convinced her there was no choice but to open the door, so she did. "Why are you here?"

He had a bag in one hand and a bottle of wine in the other. "I brought red because it's supposed to be good for the heart. And takeout food because you took care of patients all day, and I got the feeling that you needed someone to take care of you."

Self-consciously she touched her hair. "I wasn't expecting anyone."

"I know."

"And Ava's here."

"You told me."

Her insides felt warm and fuzzy, and that reaction might have had something to do with the fact that he clearly didn't expect anything in return for this kindness.

"Come in," she said, pulling the door wide.

"I brought chicken parmesan, spaghetti and meatballs. Turns out the new restaurant has takeout." He set the bag on the table beside the open container of ice cream, then gave her a "really?" look.

She shrugged. "Don't judge."

"Heaven forbid. I know where the plates are." He started to pull out three.

"Ava's already eaten."

"Okay." He got everything ready, then took aluminum containers from the bag. "It's still warm."

For a girl who had fended for herself and Ava when she was still just a kid, this being taken care of was irresistibly sweet. And without warning, her emotions spilled over.

"Okay. Let's eat—" Gabe took one look at her and said, "Court?"

She shrugged helplessly as tears rolled down her cheeks. "It's just—this is so nice of you. I had a horrible day. Three patients coded and—" She was looking at him but moisture blurred her vision. "We lost a teenage boy—"

"Oh man." In a heartbeat, he was there, wrapping her in his arms. He just held her close, rubbed her back and maybe kissed her hair. "I don't know what to say except that really sucks."

"Yup." She rested her cheek against his chest and allowed herself to accept comfort. It was selfish because this wasn't real. But didn't she deserve at least this much?

When she couldn't cry anymore, he held her at arm's length. "I'm going to pour you some wine, and you're going to tell me what happened."

A protest formed in her head, but that was as far as it got. She accepted the glass he held out, and the words started to flow as freely as her tears.

"He was only seventeen. Paramedics brought him to the ER with a drug overdose. They were doing chest compressions. He was put on a ventilator, stabilized and admitted for cardiac observation. His parents got there, and then—" The memory of the fear in their faces stopped her, but she swallowed and went on. "He coded again, and I had to handle protocols until the doctor got there. Respiratory therapy was with him, thank God." She met his gaze and wondered if she looked as horrified as she felt. "I had to get his parents out of the room. We needed space to work. Family is a distraction, but—"

"You did your job."

"Yeah. But his mom and dad weren't there when he died. I had to remove the monitors and clean him up for them to see him." She sighed. "I've lost patients before, but this got to me. It could have been Ava—"

"No." He shook his head.

"How can you be so sure?"

"I just am."

She let out a breath. "I just couldn't wait to get home and hug her."

"That's a perfectly natural reaction." He cupped her face in his hands and kissed her gently. "I'm so sorry that happened."

"Thanks. Me, too." She drew in a deep, shuddering breath. "I appreciate you listening."

"Feel better?"

"Yes. And suddenly I'm starving."

"Okay. Let's eat," he said.

They sat at the table and dug into the chicken parmesan. "This is good," she said.

"Yeah." He was looking thoughtful about something. "Ava is a really good kid."

"She is." After taking a sip of wine, she said, "But how do you know?"

"She came in for tutoring and wouldn't have if she didn't care about anything. Recently she brought someone with her. A boy. Kind of scruffy-looking, hair too long. Hostile attitude. Smart."

"Should I be worried?" *Please say no*, she silently begged.

"I checked him out with one of the teachers. Seems he's okay."

Courtney realized that he was feeling protective of Ava, like something a father might feel. It looked very cute on him, she thought. Again she had that warm and fuzzy feeling in the pit of her stomach. But why should she believe it was real?

The last time a man pretended to be a father to Ava, the whole thing had been a lie. Even though she was a willing participant in this charade with Gabe, what they were doing was a lie, too.

She looked at the stairway to make sure they were alone, then said, "You know, we have to think about ending our dating soon." Again with the air quotes.

He met her gaze, and there was something in his that was dark and indecipherable. "Really? Things are going pretty well, don't you think? My family has left me alone. Is something going on with Ava?"

"Only that she thinks I need to go steady. She's pretty vocal about wanting my boyfriend to be you, though."

"But you have misgivings about it?" He was studying her intently.

He wasn't wrong, she thought, but not for the reason he might think. Her feelings were drifting out of the neutral zone and into a very gray area that they'd cordoned off. His obviously protective streak for Ava had shown her what a real relationship could look like. Not to mention that she was starting to really dislike her new companion, guilt. It had begun to weigh on her a lot.

"Yes, I have doubts. Don't you?" she asked.

"Well, I don't have a child, so there's that. And from my perspective, this is working pretty well. But we agreed in the beginning that either of us could end it at any time for any reason. Is that what you want to do?"

"Saying yes would make me look pretty ungrateful after you brought food and wine and a shoulder to cry on." *A very nice, strong shoulder*, she thought.

"And apparently Ava doesn't suspect anything."

Courtney glanced over her own shoulder, making sure they were still alone. "No."

"Then, if you agree, I think we can put off our 'breakup' just a little bit longer."

"Okay," she said. "But I think we need to start planning it soon."

In fact, she wasn't entirely sure they hadn't already waited too long. There was her anticipation to see him tonight along with remembering the pleasure they'd shared in her bed. Not an air quote in sight when she'd been in his arms. What he made her feel was very real.

And tonight. The way he'd brought food and wine and listened. He'd held her when she cried, for goodness' sake. All of that made her feel better. Was it a lie? Going on with this too much longer was taking a huge chance. With her heart.

Gabe was leaning back in the chair behind his desk, listening to Jim Whitmire on speakerphone as he pitched him a corporate turnaround for his company. It wasn't easy to concentrate with Courtney on his mind. A couple of days ago, he'd brought her takeout Italian and held her while she cried for a teenager gone way too soon. He wasn't proud to admit that she'd felt way too good in his arms. It wasn't clear whether that was a good thing or a warning sign.

"So, what do you think?" the CFO asked.

Busted. Time for some verbal two-step. "I looked at the financial reports you sent and estimate twelve to eighteen months before implemented changes will positively affect your bottom line. Maybe longer."

"Whatever it takes," Jim vowed. "There's more at stake here than money. This is a family-owned business, so it's personal."

"Understood. The thing is, I've been kicking around the idea of starting my own company and where to put the home office."

"You could do both here," the other man suggested. "Research this area while you're working for my company."

"True. Right now I'm working in Southern California. You're on the East Coast." Gabe was thinking out loud. He was in his office, and movement in the doorway caught his eye. Aunt Lil was standing there. "I've actually considered setting up my corporate headquarters there, believe it or not."

"So, if you take us on as a client, it could be a kill-two-birds-with-one-stone scenario."

He knew his aunt was staring at him and refused to meet her gaze. But his "you're in trouble" sense was tingling. "Realistically, I couldn't start for a while. I'm still working for a company here in Huntington Hills."

"Look, Gabe, I'll take anything I can get. You come highly recommended, and terms like *the best* have been liberally thrown around where you're concerned. We can work together long-distance, at first, on a limited basis. I can structure the contract that way. Your broad recommendations to stop the hemorrhaging of cash on this end would help a lot until you're in a position to take over temporarily as CEO."

Gabe leaned forward. "You've given me a lot to consider, Jim. Send me your business plan and the most recent financials. I'll see if I can get clarity on the numbers for you."

"Clarity is going to be scary as hell," the other man admitted.

"I know, but it's necessary."

"Okay. Thanks, Gabe. I appreciate any input you

can give me. And I sincerely hope you'll come on board."

"Talk to you soon, Jim." He hung up the phone and stood, coming around the desk to rest a hip against the edge. Finally he met his aunt's gaze. "So what do you say to me taking you to lunch?"

"That is a shameless and transparent attempt to distract me, Gabriel."

"It's after noon, and I'm hungry. I'm not completely clear about what I'm distracting you from." That response could be characterized as evasive, but it was mostly a lie. And when had he gotten so good at it? Thoughts of Courtney flashed through his mind. Yup, that's when it started. And she was as uncomfortable with it as he was.

"Don't be dense, dear. It doesn't suit you at all." She moved closer to the desk and folded her arms over her chest. "You don't want to talk about what I just overheard you say to Jim on the East Coast. That's why you're playing dumb."

"Dumb?"

She tilted her head to the side. "You were discussing a job."

"Oh, that." He waved a hand dismissively. "A company is in trouble."

"I got that," she said wryly.

"This guy did some research on turnaround specialists, and my name came up. It was no big deal."

"You're thinking about starting your own consulting company. That's pertinent information."

"Yes. But you already know that," he reminded

her. "I talked to you about it when you asked for my help with Make Me a Match."

"You've been freelancing and never said a word about corporate headquarters. That implies hiring people to work for you and doing it on the other side of the country."

"That's my plan. But I haven't made any decisions yet on where it will be. The East Coast isn't that far." He shrugged.

"Last time I checked, it was a pretty long plane ride. Why not just go for Micronesia?" Lillian Gordon was normally the voice of calm in the center of chaos. Rational and serene. She wasn't that way now.

"This is all in the talking stage, Aunt Lil."

"I know you pretty well, Gabriel. You have a tell when your mind is all but made up. If the words come out of your mouth, it's a very good bet that your brain has filtered them first." Her eyes narrowed on him. "I thought you were sticking around for good."

"Did I ever say that?" he countered.

"You said you were okay with the idea of putting the brakes on your career to help me."

"If I remember correctly, I said that brakes on my career would give me a chance to figure out my next professional move." He pointed at her. "You have selective interpretation, Aunt Lil."

"Potato, po-tah-to." She huffed out a breath. "I had the distinct impression that you were staying in Huntington Hills."

"I never said that." But he didn't quite look her in the eyes, because he knew what he would see there.

"You're right. I did read between the lines," she admitted. "Because you are very dear to me and I very much like having you around."

He met her gaze then and, sure enough, it was there. Disappointment. Was there anyone, anywhere, who didn't hate seeing that look on the face of someone they respected and loved? He thought not and was no exception.

"You know the most recent numbers for Make Me a Match are very good. That could mean a lucrative buyout offer. I've gotten a few calls," he admitted. "Companies are reaching out with proposals that would assure you're more than comfortable for the rest of your life. You could retire with peace of mind."

"What if I'm not ready to retire?" She was pouting.

"If the deal is negotiated shrewdly, you could stay on as a consultant for as long as you want."

"That could be attractive," she acknowledged. "But you are trying to distract me again."

And it nearly worked, he thought. "It's just something to think about."

"And I will," she promised. "Along with mulling over why in the world you would even consider a job that would take you so far away. Your mother is so happy to have all her children close by. As am I. And we were relieved to see you finally putting down roots. Why would you go to the other side of the country?"

"For one thing," he said, "it would be next to

impossible for my mother to interfere in my life. I wouldn't have to attend Sunday dinners where someone in the family has invited a woman to fix me up with."

"Seriously? That's it? That's your reasoning?" She shook her head as if he was a dimwit. "Don't you see? We don't have to find women for you anymore because you have Courtney now. She's such a lovely young woman."

He was in complete agreement about that. A vision instantly formed in his mind of her just a few nights ago. In sweatpants, an old T-shirt, freshly washed hair and no makeup. She certainly hadn't been trying to impress him because she didn't know he was going to show up. But he found her captivating.

He wanted her.

Then his aunt's words sank in. The family had backed off throwing women at him. That meant they completely bought in to his fake relationship with Courtney.

Courtney had just said they needed to end it soon. Something in her eyes when she did had made him uneasy. Part of him, a very big part, had pushed back at the suggestion. But, per their verbal agreement, if everyone believed they cared, the meddlers would be forced to give them time to mourn when it was over. This conversation with his aunt was proof they'd reached their goal and crossed the finish line. Fake dating had produced the desired outcome.

His aunt cleared her throat to get his attention. "Say something, Gabriel."

"Courtney is special." It was a relief not to have to lie.

"I agree. And if you take a job on the other side of the country, what about her? Women like her don't grow on trees, you know. And I haven't seen you this happy since before Margo died."

Happy? Really? Couldn't she see he was still angry about what fate took from him?

Gabe stared at her, waiting for the heat of anger to swell inside him and fill up the painfully lonely and empty spaces. But nothing happened. It didn't come. The simmering bitterness wasn't there. He tried to remember the last time a surge of fury had overwhelmed him and couldn't.

Uneasiness had him wondering when he'd last made a concentrated effort to recall Margo's voice. He hadn't been sure that was even possible, but he used to take a stab at it anyway. But not recently. The realization rocked him that he hadn't tried to see her face in his memories, either.

The only face he instantly saw now was Courtney's. The night she'd called off their dinner date, he'd heard distress and sadness in her voice. There was no way he wasn't going to her. He was a fixer, and he couldn't ignore the instinct telling him she was broken.

Suddenly the triple whammy hit him squarely in the chest. The three amigos, his stalwart companions since burying his wife—pain, survivor's guilt and grief. But the anger he'd always used as a shield was gone. There was nothing standing between him and the feelings of loss he'd stubbornly refused to acknowledge. Courtney had penetrated that armor, and now he could add betrayal of those memories to the list of his sins.

Chapter Twelve

"Is Mr. B coming over tonight?"

Courtney carried two totes of groceries through the door from her garage to the kitchen. She glanced over her shoulder at Ava, who was helping lug the stuff. "I don't think so."

"But it's Saturday night, and you're off this weekend."

"That doesn't mean we are obligated to see each other."

"But you're dating," her daughter reminded her.

They were "dating," with air quotes, Courtney thought. "And sometimes people are too busy to go out."

Ava put her bags on the kitchen table. "It's just that I went for tutoring this week, and he said something about going to the pier at the beach. So, I was wondering if you're going to be seeing him some-time this weekend."

Courtney had been pleased and surprised when Ava actually volunteered to go to the market with her. She missed the days when her little girl always wanted to go "bye-bye." Now she was beginning to think there was an underlying motivation and just had to figure out what was going on.

She put a half gallon of milk in the refrigerator and a replacement ice cream container in the freezer. Sometimes with Ava the direct approach worked. "Is there something on your mind, sweetie?"

"No." But the single word sounded a lot like a question.

Rome wasn't built in a day, she thought, hold-ing back a sigh. "So you've been going to tutoring."

"Yeah." A bag of chips crackled as Ava pulled it open. She popped one in her mouth and started to talk.

Courtney was about to issue the usual mom direc-tive to not carry on a conversation with her mouth full but didn't have to.

"I know," Ava said with her hand covering the lower half of her face while she chewed. "Sorry."

Persistence paid off. Good to know. When the coast was clear, she said to the teen, "You were say-ing?"

"Mr. B is a good tutor. He makes math fun and easier to understand." She pulled another chip out of the bag but didn't eat it. "I got a B plus on my algebra test."

"Wow." Courtney's heart swelled with pride in her offspring, and she thought she just might explode with it. "Congratulations. See, hard work really does pay off."

"Yeah. I get it." Ava was trying to put on her sullen "don't lecture me" face, but a smile leaked out. "I held up my end of the bargain."

"What bargain is that? You're not grounded and haven't been for a while. I'm dating." Mentally she added air quotes to that last word and crossed her fingers behind her back, hoping the half-truth wouldn't deduct too many points from her positive karma. It was time for a lateral subject change. "Gabe told me you showed up at tutoring with a boy."

"Yeah. Nick Perino."

His name had come up when they were talking about the cute boy that made you want to go to school every day. Courtney waited for more, but the teen stuffed a chip in her mouth. *Persistence*, she reminded herself. "Tell me about him."

"What did Mr. B say?"

"That his attitude could be better and he badly needed a haircut."

"Mom—"

She held up a hand. "He also said Nick is really smart. He doesn't need extra math help but apparently is willing to go to tutoring just to spend time with you. My takeaway is that if you're his friend, he must be okay."

"He is."

The glow on her daughter's face was both beautiful and worrisome. Every fiber of Courtney's being, every bit of energy she possessed, was about protecting this child she'd created. She never knew if she was doing the right thing, saying something to push her away. And her own dysfunctional family experience didn't give her a foundation for a solid maternal skill set. Gabe had hit the family lottery with his, and she envied him that. Still, she never wanted to look back and regret *not* saying something to Ava about choices.

"How much do you like this boy?" A dark cloud of hostility chased away Ava's glow, and Courtney hastily added, "I'm not prying—" She stopped, because that's exactly what she was doing. "Delete that. It's just that I know from experience that guys tell you what you want to hear, promise the moon and really only want one thing—"

"Sex."

Courtney cleared her throat. "Yes."

"I haven't had sex," Ava said defiantly.

"I'm not saying that. I know you're only fourteen." But she believed her. "It never hurts to have an honest discussion, a reminder about birth control. Because I also know how big feelings are at your age. I just want to say again that you can always come to me about anything. I won't judge."

"Right." There was skepticism in Ava's expression.

"I will always do my level best not to judge," she amended.

"Okay, Mom."

"The thing is, sweetie, I just love you so much. I want the best for you. When you're happy, I'm happy. And I will always do what I think is right to keep you that way."

Ava closed up the bag of chips and put a clip on it. "So, since we're having an honest discussion, how much do you like Mr. B? Remember, be truthful."

Where Gabe was concerned, honesty was a slippery slope. "That's a good question—"

"Do not tell me you'll think about it and get back to me," Ava warned.

"What makes you think I was going to do that?" Besides the fact that it was exactly what she'd planned to do.

"Since I was a little girl and asked a question or permission to go somewhere, do something that you were uncomfortable with, that's been your standard response." She huffed out a breath and jammed a hand on her hip, a stubborn pose that looked awfully familiar.

"Ava—"

"I'm asking because I love you, too, Mom. When you're happy, I'm happy. And I want to keep you that way," her diabolical child repeated back to her. "Seriously, it's not a hard question."

It was for her where Gabe was concerned. "How do you feel about him?"

"Mom—" Exasperation turned Ava's voice into a near whine. "You always tell me not to answer a question with another question."

"I have a very good reason for asking," she defended. "As you well know, any decision I make about letting a man into my life will directly affect yours."

Ava rolled her eyes, walked to the cupboard, pulled out a glass, then filled it with filtered water from the refrigerator. She took a drink, but that didn't cool the hot anger in her eyes. "You're talking about the Adam."

"Yes."

"The one who showed me your engagement ring to get my permission before he proposed to you and promised to be a dad to me. And—" She paused for dramatic effect. "The same ass who obviously wanted a family but only kids who were his."

"Yeah, that's the jerk I mean." Courtney would never forgive herself for the awful episode and her horrific lapse in judgment about men. She'd vowed it would not happen again. It was the motivation for her agreement with Gabe. Like he'd said, a protection for both of them.

Ava wanted her to date, and that's what she was doing. But the situation was taking a turn toward complicated, and she was flying by the seat of her pants here.

"Why are you bringing this up now?" she asked her daughter.

"I saw you the other night. When he brought over the Italian food."

Thoughts of that night made her feel warm and gooey inside. It was such a sweet thing to do. She couldn't remember if anyone had ever held her when she cried. And she'd believed they were alone. "You saw us?"

Ava nodded. "I was coming downstairs to say hello to him. Then I saw him hugging you, and I felt weird. I didn't want to interrupt."

Had they said anything about fake dating? Anything Ava had heard? "Did you hear what we were saying?"

"You weren't talking. I just heard you crying. Why were you?"

Courtney didn't talk about the hospital very much, partly because of patient privacy issues, partly to keep the bad things from Ava. There was so much that could affect her, and she was at such an impressionable age. But she couldn't keep everything away, and this might be one of the times to share.

"A boy came into the hospital. A drug overdose. He didn't make it. That upset me very much."

"Because of me," Ava guessed. "And that's why you canceled dinner with Mr. B."

"Yes. I was so sad about a young life cut short. His parents—what they're going through is unimaginable to me. And I don't ever want to know. You think I lecture, but sweetie, I just worry so much about you. One stupid decision and—"

"I know." Ava put down her water, then stepped into Courtney's arms. "And I knew something was bothering you. I'm glad he came over and fed you. You seemed better after that."

"I was. It helped." And then she'd told him they should end this charade soon.

"So boys only want one thing." Ava moved away, and there was a gleam in her eyes.

Courtney knew she was going to regret saying that. "It's the rumor."

"Did you and Mr. B ever have sex?"

That was not a question she was prepared to answer, and her mind raced. It was like tripping and trying to catch yourself with nothing to grab onto. You knew it was going to be bad when any part of your body hit the ground.

The best response she could come up with was "That's not really important." Hey, it was better than *none of your business*.

"So, that's a big fat yes." Ava's smile was triumphant, although not in a bad way. "It never hurts to have a reminder about birth control."

Courtney sighed. "The good news is your words are positive proof that you actually listen to me."

"And the bad news?" Her teen shrugged. "There always is."

"You're too darn smart for your own good. And my peace of mind."

"So, you love Mr. B."

She stared at her daughter and managed to choke out, "Wait, what?"

"You keep telling me that I should be in love if I have sex. That means you must be in love with him," Ava concluded.

Well, damn. Should she have seen this coming?

When two people dated for a certain length of time, did everyone automatically assume they were sleeping together? Advice to this kid about love and sex was sound, even if her "relationship" didn't bear that out.

"How do you feel about him?" Courtney had asked this a few minutes ago, but Ava had evaded answering. She waited for a pushback now, but it didn't come.

"I like him a lot," she said enthusiastically. "He's a good guy, honest and says what he means. You could do a lot worse."

In fact, she had.

"He *is* a good guy and so far has told the truth," Courtney admitted.

About everything but the true nature of their "relationship." But Courtney was in on that. More concerning to her now was the fact that Ava seemed to be starting to count on him. Her instincts the other night to end things were right on.

But, wow, she realized she didn't want to. She wasn't in love with him, but she would never have slept with him if she didn't have positive feelings. And he seemed to like her, too. There was genuine concern when he came over with food and the comfort of his arms. Wouldn't she know if he was pretending?

She was tired of putting air quotes in every thought she had about Gabe and every comment she made about him. Maybe it was possible that he wanted to remove them, too.

* * *

On Monday at work, Courtney was in the hospital cafeteria eating her lunch when Taylor sat down at her table.

"Is it my imagination," her friend said, "or are Mondays busier and more hectic than other days of the week?"

"In your department, babies come when they come." Courtney speared a piece of lettuce with her fork. "But it always feels that way, doesn't it? My judgment is off, though, after the bad day I had last week. We lost a kid. Seventeen."

"Oh man—" There was instant sympathy in the other woman's eyes. "I'm sorry, Court. That had to hit a nerve for you."

"Yeah. It really got to me. I canceled dinner with Gabe. Just not very good company."

"How did he take it?" Taylor met her gaze and shrugged. "How a man takes rejection says a lot about him. Even if you do have a prior agreement."

"There was no rejection. What we have is all for show." Tell that to her quivering hormones. "I told him I had a bad day, and why, then asked for a rain check." Remembering what happened next made her smile.

"Why are you looking like that, all shiny and glowing? What did he do?"

Courtney finished the last bite of salad and set her fork down before wiping her mouth with a napkin. Deliberately drawing out the reveal drove her friend crazy, but she couldn't resist.

"Come on, Court. I can't stand the suspense." She took a bite of her tuna melt and chewed while staring expectantly.

"Thirty minutes after I called him, he came over with a bottle of wine and takeout from the new restaurant where we were going to go. He said I needed taking care of."

"Oh—" Taylor's mouth was full so she couldn't say more, but she made approving sounds to go with her favorable and mushy expression. After swallowing, she said in a reproving tone, "Courtney—"

"What?"

"You need to hang on to that man."

"No. It wouldn't be fair to him. This charade was his idea. His wife died, and he doesn't want to get serious. I understand that, because I don't, either."

"Sometimes serious just happens when you're not looking or expecting it." There was an "am I right?" look on her friend's face.

"I can't do that to him. What we have is an insurance policy to avoid getting hurt. The rules are in place."

"Rules were made to be broken," Taylor pointed out. "Unless, of course, Ava doesn't like him."

"We had a discussion just recently about that very thing." She sipped her iced tea. "She wanted to know how I felt about him."

"And you told her…" Impatience glittered in her friend's green eyes.

"It was a complicated conversation."

"Why? It's a yes or no question."

"Somehow the subject of sex came up." The question still made her uncomfortable. "And she made a huge leap that I'm in love with Gabe."

"You slept with him?" Taylor's mouth formed an O.

Courtney winced. "Why don't you say that louder? I don't think they heard you on the fourth floor."

Taylor glanced around the busy lunch-hour cafeteria. People were moving around, talking, banging trays and utensils against plates. "No one heard me. Now quit stalling and answer the question."

"I don't want to. You're going to get judge-y and jump to conclusions."

"Have you met me?" She looked exasperated. "I'm the queen of live and let live. The empress of nice work if you can get it. *And* your best friend."

"Okay. I'm sorry. This is just hard to say." She lowered her voice. "Yes, I slept with him."

"And?"

"It was magical." She could still remember the feel of his lips on hers. Memories of him touching her everywhere haunted her dreams. "I would do it again in a heartbeat."

"Then there's your answer. The two of you have already changed the rules. Take the natural next step. Dip a toe in the water and tell him you are down with complications."

"I don't know—" Courtney caught her bottom lip between her teeth.

"What have you got to lose? There was an expiration date on this pretense from the beginning, so it will be over anyway. Don't think of it as changing the rules."

"But it is."

"Think of it as being honest," Taylor suggested.

That would be different, Courtney thought. But what if it went badly? That was the pessimist in her. The optimist reminded her that he was the one who had said they could put off the end a little longer. If they did, she could have more days with him, like the recent trip to the pier. Her and Gabe and Ava laughing, playing carnival games and riding the carousel. His big, steady hand holding hers. Opening doors for her and Ava, showing her daughter what a good man looked like. One who regularly got a haircut.

The idea was irresistibly tempting, but somehow she stood firm. "There's nothing wrong with not rocking the boat."

"That's the difference between you and me." Taylor's voice held a note of irritation. "I believe in being proactive. Wondering what might have been isn't for me."

"That's because you proactively push guys away before they can hurt you."

"Maybe," Taylor admitted. "But no one has to wonder where they stand."

"True." Courtney glanced at the watch on her wrist. "Wow, I have to go."

"Okay. And, Court—" Taylor's expression was apologetic. "Didn't mean to push. It's just that he sounds like such a great guy. You know I just want you to be happy, right?"

"I know. It's fine. All good. I'll talk to you soon."

Courtney emptied her trash into the garbage and stacked the tray with the others on top, then headed out of the cafeteria. Not far down the hall on her right was a bank of elevators, and she took one up to the fourth floor, where the cardiac observation unit was located. The nursing supervisor alerted her to a newly admitted patient, and she went to the room after checking the medical notes.

She walked into the room and glanced at the dry-erase board with the patient's name, her doctor, an emergency contact and the nurse taking care of her today. That would be Courtney.

"Hi, Linda, my name is Courtney, and I'm your nurse. How are you feeling?"

"Okay." The patient had an IV and was hooked up to a heart monitor. She looked small in the bed, and her short, dark hair was streaked with silver. The chart said she was fifty-eight.

"So you came in to the emergency room with chest pain."

The woman nodded. "They drew blood and I had an echo something."

"Echocardiogram," Courtney said. "We're waiting on the results now."

"Yes. The doctor said depending on what it says, he might want to do more tests. I forget what."

"Probably a heart catheterization."

"That sounds right." Linda looked tired and some-what uninterested. Aloof.

"Have you been sleeping well?"

"An hour here and there. Two days ago I lost someone—" Her mouth trembled, and she pressed her lips together.

"I'm so sorry. It's hard losing a spouse—"

"We weren't married. Talking about it, though. He was the love of my life."

Courtney had learned talking helped, and she was there to listen and observe. "How did you meet him—"

"Frank," she said. "We were high school sweet-hearts. So much in love it hurt as only teenagers can be."

"And you never married?"

"Not to each other." An infinitely sad look slid into her eyes. "We had a fight over something stu-pid. I can't even remember what it was about. But we broke up."

"I see from the board over there that you have a daughter. She's your emergency contact."

"Lori." She smiled. "I met someone in college and married him. Frank married, too, and had a family. Neither of the marriages worked out, and we stayed too long, trying not to fail. For the kids."

"I understand that." *All too well*, Courtney thought and still regretted it.

"Eventually Frank and I found each other again. We realized that we never stopped loving each other, and now he's gone. We wasted so many years, so much time we could have been together, loving each other." Her eyes filled with tears. "He had a massive heart attack. The paramedics couldn't revive him."

"I'm so sorry you're going through this." Courtney was holding her hand and squeezed it reassuringly.

Just then Dr. Shows walked into the room. The cardiologist wore a white lab coat over his blue scrubs. "Hi, Mrs. Kearny. How are you feeling? Any more chest pain?"

"No. I'm comfortable now. But you're probably here to tell me I had a heart attack."

"The tests so far don't confirm that. There are no cardiac enzymes in your blood, and the echocardiogram showed severe left-ventricle systolic dysfunction. The wall motion pattern present suggests stress-induced cardiomyopathy."

"Translation? In English, please." Linda smiled.

"It doesn't look like a heart attack," he said.

Courtney's job was to give him all the facts. She worked with Dr. Shows a lot and had for quite a while. She respected him, partly because he'd learned to trust her instincts and judgment. "Linda was just telling me she recently experienced an emotional upset. Lost someone very dear to her."

He met her gaze, and his eyes said he understood where she was going with this. "You're thinking broken heart syndrome."

"What's that?" the woman asked. "Other than the obvious."

"More times than I can count, I've told a patient

they're having a coronary due to a thrombus in the artery and we need to do an angiogram to open the vessel and restore blood flow. And then have to eat my words, because the arteries were normal."

"So it's not a heart attack?"

"We'll go ahead and do the angio to make sure, but because of your recent trauma and the negative tests we've done, there's a good chance that it's not. If I'm right about this, normal function usually returns after one to four weeks on medication. Beta-blockers and, temporarily, ACE inhibitors."

"That's good news, then," Linda said.

"Potentially. I want that test before I say definitively."

"But this news will help you relax a little," Courtney pointed out.

"Yes. Thank you, Doctor," Linda said.

"Of course. I'm going to schedule the angio. In the meantime, get some rest." He nodded his thanks to Courtney, then walked out of the room.

"So," Courtney said, "you must be feeling a little better about things."

"Yes and no. I'm not scared for my health, just about the future. Being alone. Lonely. Grieving. Learning to live without Frank."

"You have your daughter." Courtney couldn't think of anything else comforting to say.

"Yes." Linda's eyes were dark and a little vacant when she looked at Courtney. "Are you married?"

"Divorced."

"Seeing anyone?"

Courtney wasn't sure how to answer that and finally said, "I've had a few dates recently."

"Do you like him?"

Thoughts of Gabe made her smile, and her pulse sprinted into a hundred-yard dash. "Yes."

"Soul-deep love is rare, Courtney. If you find it, don't blow it. Grab on to it with both hands—" A tear rolled down her cheek.

"You should get some rest, Linda. I'll be back in a little while to check on you."

"Thank you." Her eyes closed.

Quietly, Courtney slipped out of the room, but she couldn't get the woman's words out of her mind. Her job involved caring for critically ill patients, and almost all of them talked about needing more time. Or if they'd known then what they knew now, things would have been different. Since Gabriel, the words resonated with her in a way they never did before.

First Taylor urged her to take a chance, and now this woman who'd lost a love and had a physical reaction to it. Gabriel Blackburne was a special man, capable of deep love. She couldn't help wondering if they could have something real, something without air quotes. When the universe was sending you signs, it didn't seem wise to ignore them.

She was going to find out.

Chapter Thirteen

After talking to his aunt, Gabe had figured two years was long enough to avoid dealing with his loss. In some ways he already had, but it was superficial. Like not expecting to see Margo when he came home from work late at night. He'd even passed the stage where he wasn't consciously thinking about her. Then he'd forget he didn't expect to see her and feel the slice of pain in his chest when he realized all over again that she wasn't there and he was alone. But he never slowed down in his work long enough to deal with what being alone meant.

Not until Courtney.

Because they had to put on their "dating" faces, technically he wasn't alone. If he was being honest, this farce with her was the most alive he'd felt in a long time. She was fun, and he looked forward to seeing her. He let himself enjoy time with her because he didn't have to worry about where this was going. The indefiniteness of it was genius, if he did say so himself.

"Gabe?" Courtney sat at a right angle to him at her kitchen table. "I don't think you heard a word I just said."

"Hmm?" He blinked at her and came back to the present. It was Saturday night, and he was at her place for a quiet dinner. "I'm sorry. What did you say?"

"Apparently nothing of great consequence." Courtney looked at Ava, who was sitting across the table from her. The teen had joined them for dinner, which was a pleasant surprise. "You, my dear daughter, are officially no longer the only one who doesn't listen to me."

Gabe bumped the fist the teen held out to him. He needed to be present right now and not thinking about the past. There would be plenty of time to do that later, when he was alone.

"Wow, Courtney, this is the best meat loaf I've ever tasted. You have outdone yourself."

"Oh, dude, you caved. That's lame. Very not cool." Ava gave him a pitying look. "Who has the upper hand in this relationship, anyway? You have to stay strong."

"Our 'relationship'—" He briefly met Courtney's gaze and saw the sparkle of their secret in her eyes and the wink of her dimples as she tried not to smile.

"—is based on mutual respect and compromise. I was so wrapped up in the deliciousness of this dinner that nothing penetrated my concentration."

Courtney laughed. "Ava's right. Lame. And it's really all right to be distracted."

"Okay. From now on I'll leave work at the office." It wasn't a total lie. He had sort of been thinking about work and how it kept him from dealing with his personal loss.

"Can I ask one question?" Courtney said.

He nodded. "Shoot."

"How's your aunt's business? Is Make Me a Match doing better?"

"It is," he confirmed. "Even better than I'd hoped. We're going to look at hiring another full-time employee. In fact, we're discussing what our needs are in order to put together the job description."

"That's great."

"Yeah." That conversation with his aunt hadn't been far from his mind for the last couple of weeks. And he was pretty sure it was responsible for his being distracted now. He'd paused his career to bail her out and now had to make decisions about his own future. That dredged up stuff from his past—hence the dark thoughts.

"Is it? Great, I mean?" Courtney was studying him as if not quite buying the positive business news he was selling.

Ava's sounds of impatience interrupted the conversation before her mom could explain. The teen was following house rules by putting her phone on vibrate at dinner and not looking at it. But the thing had been buzzing at regular intervals throughout the meal. "Mom, please can I check messages now?"

"Permission granted. Because you were so gracious about a Saturday night dinner with us."

"I'm glad you were here to take my side," Gabe told her. "Thanks for having my back."

"Any time, Mr. B."

"I'm tough. I can handle you two ganging up on me." Courtney grinned at both of them.

Gabe felt that smile deep in his gut, and the fact that it got to him hit a nerve. One that had been exposed ever since the day his aunt overheard him talking about leaving town. One of her first questions had been "What about Courtney?" He'd felt a completely involuntary, gut-level flash of not wanting to leave her. That wasn't supposed to happen.

"Mom, can I go to Lexi's house and spend the night?"

"Who else will be there?"

"Just Becca and Amy."

Courtney nodded that she knew and approved of them. "Are her parents going to be there?"

"Yes." Barely suppressed frustration and annoyance wrapped around the single word.

Courtney met his gaze for a second, but there was a definite gleam in hers that said, "We'll be all alone and whatever should we do?" The thought of being alone with her naked in his arms made him ache for her.

"Then I don't see why you can't go to Lexi's,"

Courtney said. "Remember we're going to Gabe's mom's house tomorrow for Sunday dinner. You need to be home early enough to clean up for that."

"Will the twins be there?" Ava wanted to know.

"No one misses dinner at my mom's unless they're sick or out of state," Gabe said. The out-of-state excuse might exempt him soon. He felt another twinge in his chest, but it felt like regret, and that was unacceptable. It was a violation of their bargain.

"I really like your family," Ava said to him.

"They like you, too." He looked at her fresh, innocent face and realized, not for the first time, that he really liked this kid. He envied Courtney the experience of being her mother. And there was a flash of guilt for pulling her into the Blackburne family when he knew it would only last for a finite amount of time. And he got another one of those gut-level flashes of not wanting this to go away.

"Okay." Ava stood and typed a quick text into her phone. "I'm going to throw some stuff together. Becca's mom is picking me up on the way."

"Okay."

The teen started to leave the room, then stopped. "Mr. B, I have that big algebra test next week. Can you still do an extra tutoring session with me?"

"Yeah. I've already cleared it with Brett—Mr. Kamp. I'll meet you in his classroom on the day we agreed. One on one to make sure you'll ace that exam."

"Thanks." Spontaneously, she bent and gave him a hug. "You're the best."

No, he wasn't. Not even close. And the thought produced more than a sprinkling of guilt for deceiving her.

Twenty minutes later, the teen's ride arrived. After a hasty goodbye, she left, and Courtney's house was unnaturally quiet.

She started clearing the table of plates, and Gabe took them from her. "I'll make you a deal."

"Another one?" Her wicked, teasing look would test the righteousness of a saint.

He was no saint. "You handle putting the leftovers away, and I'll do the dishes."

"That's the best deal I've heard in a while. More wine?" she asked.

"No, thanks."

In a short time, almost everything was tidy again except the meat-loaf pan and the big bowl used for mashed potatoes. He hand washed them because they were too big for the dishwasher; she dried them with a towel, then put them away. They worked as a team, and it felt so natural. So normal. He was feeling contentment and wondered when that had happened.

Gabe had been preoccupied with his own thoughts and didn't realize until just then that Courtney hadn't said much since her daughter left.

"What's on your mind?" he asked.

"How do you know something is?" She rested a hip against the cupboard underneath the sink and looked up at him.

How did he know? Best guess was he'd connected with her and recognized her moods now. And this one was easy. She rarely asked about his aunt's business, and something had been bothering her since she brought it up. She'd joined in the teasing after that, but he recognized her carefree expression, and this wasn't it.

Probably she wanted to discuss picking a time to end their relationship. To "break up." He hadn't changed his mind and felt they could hold off just a little longer. That was selfish, but it's how he rolled. He wanted a bit more time before he had to say goodbye to this interlude.

"I can just tell you're thinking too much," he finally said. "So tell me what's going on. We've always been able to talk."

She blew out a breath and nervously toyed with the towel in her hands. "I don't know where to start or how to say this."

"Just jump in anywhere," he suggested.

"Okay." She looked at him, and darned if there wasn't something that bore a strong resemblance to hope in her eyes. "You are a really good man. You're kind and considerate. I won't hold it against you that you don't take no for an answer when a dinner date gets canceled. That you show up with food when a girl is in her bare face and not expecting company."

"It's a flaw." He remembered that night and refusing to accept that he wouldn't be able to see her after looking forward to it all day. After her call, he'd had the feeling that she was all alone and in a dark place. He just couldn't ignore the urge to go to her and somehow fix what was wrong. "I'm working on it."

"As well you should be, mister." She cleared her throat. "The thing is, I like and respect you very much. Ava does, too."

That really made him feel good, until it didn't. Kids didn't suffer fools easily, and he hoped her daughter never learned of their plan to fool her. "You've done an amazing job with her."

"Thanks." She looked down at her hands, the dish towel still dangling from her fingers, then back up. "That night, when I was in such a crappy mood and you were here for me, I mentioned that we should think about ending things soon."

"I remember. And I said we could wait a little longer. I haven't changed my mind about that."

"Right. That's what I wanted to talk about. We've been putting it off, and maybe there's a reason for that."

"Yeah. It buys us time with our well-intentioned families so they'll give us peace."

"Yeah, that, too. But—"

"What?" he asked.

She met his gaze. "Maybe deep down neither of us wants to split up. What if we tried dating without air quotes? What if we go out for real? I like you a lot, and I believe you feel the same way about me. I'd like to find out if we could be something more than coconspirators."

Gabe was stunned into silence. She wanted to change things? Cancel their insurance policy? Explore a real relationship and open the door to getting his teeth kicked in again, emotionally speaking?

Something expanded in his chest—hot, hard, famil-iar. Well, what do you know. His old friend anger was finally putting in an appearance.

"What does 'for real' mean?" he asked slowly, coldly.

"Just how it sounds." Courtney's hopeful expres-sion turned to uncertainty. "We continue to see each other. I'm having fun with you. If you're not having fun with me, too, it's an awfully good act. What if we date? Spend time together to find out if we could be more than a fake couple."

"No." He shook his head. The shock on her face compelled him to add, "I'm not a good bet."

"I don't know what that means." Her hands stilled, and the dish towel dropped to the floor unnoticed. "What are you saying?"

"You need to know the whole truth about me. I told you Margo died, but I never mentioned she wanted more than anything to be a mother."

"Oh—"

Gabe took a step back when she reached out a hand to offer sympathy. He didn't want it. He didn't *deserve* it. "I convinced her to wait so I could take another contract, a very high-profile job. Something that would let me write my own ticket after the com-pany turned a profit. She agreed to delay getting pregnant because I wanted another business score. Fate chose to take her, but she died without know-ing what it felt like to have a child."

"It's not your fault, Gabe. We all have regrets, de-cisions we would change if we could see the future."

"I buried myself in work so I wouldn't have time to think about what a selfish bastard I am. The kind of man who ruthlessly goes after what he wants at the expense of someone else's dreams. I care about you, Courtney, too much to hurt you."

But her face gave away how thoroughly he had failed at that. There was a bruised expression in her eyes that clearly showed he'd blindsided and disillusioned her. She drew in a shuddering breath and met his gaze. He could see the effort it took to hold back tears.

"In all the time we've had this fake relationship," she said, "that's the first time you've actually lied to me. The truth is that you're afraid of being hurt again, and you're hiding from possibilities to protect yourself. The way you protected yourself with work after your wife died."

"So you're an amateur psychologist?" He could see that accusation hit pretty close to the mark. "Well, it takes one to know one. You've been using single motherhood as a shield to protect yourself. It's an excuse to not put yourself out there."

"I never said I wasn't. The difference is that you made me want to try again. But you're still using an excuse not to."

"The whole point of our agreement was not to make promises or have expectations."

"Okay, then. That answers my question. Clearly we're not fake dating anymore. If only this was a fake fight." Her voice trembled. "But it's not, and I think you should leave now."

"You're probably right."

Gabe headed for the front door and let himself out. Cold air hit him and cleared the anger away. When it was gone, he was conflicted about what had just happened. Calling it quits was the right move, obviously. But if that was true, why did he want so badly to go back inside and fix what he'd just broken between them?

Courtney didn't sleep much that night. Her feelings about Gabe swung like a pendulum, from wishing she hadn't said anything to calling him an unfeeling jerk. And, hurt as she was, she still realized that was completely unfair. The next morning, she was tired and upset, but she hadn't shed any tears. Soon Ava would be home, and she had to be told what was going on. The timing sucked, because her daughter had been looking forward to Sunday dinner with the Blackburnes. Gabe complained about his family, but clearly he loved them. They were everything she'd always wanted—for herself and Ava.

Just then the teen in her thoughts walked in the door and set her backpack at the foot of the stairs. Ava saw her sitting on the couch and said, "Mom?"

"Hi, sweetie." It was almost noon, and she was still in her pajamas. There was a mug of cold coffee on the table beside her. "Did you have fun?"

"Yeah, it was okay." She sat down and stared. "You look terrible."

"Thank you—" She tried to joke, but when the words caught in her throat, it was just pathetic.

"Are you all right?"

"Fine."

"You're not dressed yet." Ava was good at stating the obvious.

"Yeah. I didn't feel like it." She shrugged. "So I didn't."

"But what about Sunday dinner? You said I had to come home and clean up."

"About that—" Courtney's eyes filled with tears, and that took her completely by surprise. She'd been so sure she was in control.

"Mom, what is it? You hardly ever cry. This is scaring me." Ava moved closer and took her hand. "Tell me."

"I broke up with Gabe last night." Technically she'd told him to leave, so that made her the initiator of the breakup. She'd also kicked off the scenario where he had to tell her she was nothing to him except a participant in a scheme to get his family off his back. Sure, they'd had fun, but he'd said up front it wouldn't get complicated. Then she had to go and complicate everything by falling for him. Tears rolled down her cheeks.

"Oh, Mom—" Ava gathered her close. "I'm so sorry."

"Thanks, sweetie."

If there was any silver lining to this at all, it was that she didn't have to pretend to be heartbroken. Not being a very good actress, she would have had a hard time convincing her über observant daughter that she was.

Gabe was an extraordinary man, so much a gentleman, with so much love to give. There seemed to be genuine feelings between them. Courtney knew it was real, or she would never have slept with him.

"I'll be okay." She sniffled.

"But, Mom, what happened?" Ava was perplexed. "When I left last night, you two were teasing and flirting. I'm sure there was sex."

"Not so much." There probably would have been, but she'd pushed for more. And he wasn't over losing his wife. "I thought there was a chance that we could be more than friends, but he made it clear that was never going to happen."

"So he was just another guy who said whatever it took to get what he wanted." Ava's voice vibrated with anger.

"No, sweetie." Courtney heaved a big sigh and pulled herself together. She scooted forward on the couch and looked at the last gasp of innocence fading from her daughter's face. "Gabe isn't like that. It's not his fault he doesn't feel the same way about me."

"Yes, it is. You're awesome. Beautiful and funny and a great mom. He's a jerk for not seeing all of that."

"Not a jerk. Just a guy who loved his wife and lost her unexpectedly." Courtney knew he'd been devastated when Margo died. She'd seen it in his eyes when they first met, when he told her why he didn't have kids. And last night he'd confessed that he had a lot of guilt for not having a baby when she wanted one. He was punishing himself for something that wasn't his fault. "He doesn't ever want to love some-one again because that would risk him getting hurt."

"That's just stupid. If you have a chance to be happy, you should take it." Ava's tone was scathing. "If he wasn't looking for someone ever, why did he even ask you out? It's not right to lead someone on like that. He's a horrible man. If that's the way he feels, he should have been honest in the beginning. Put it all out there before letting you get emotionally involved. It's just mean."

"Relationships aren't that simple. Never black-and-white." She and Gabe had started out that way. Everything spelled out, a plan in place. It was going to be fun, maybe a little payback for the meddlers in their lives. Very quickly her feelings had grown into something more. That wasn't on him. Courtney couldn't help herself. He was the nicest, most decent man she'd ever met.

She took Ava's hand between her own and real-ized it was shaking. "He's not to blame. I promise you that. It's not his fault."

"It is his fault," Ava cried. "If he doesn't want a family, he shouldn't have asked you out in the first place. Because you and I are a family. It was wrong of him. And I'm never going to believe anything a guy tells me. Not ever again. Love is a big trap, and I'm not doing it. I hate him."

"No—"

"Don't stick up for him, Mom. He's not a good guy. How can you not hate him, too? Why are you defending him?"

Courtney couldn't let Ava believe this about Gabe. If she didn't have all the facts about what went wrong, this experience could affect Ava's attitude about men for the rest of her life. This plan was supposed to salvage her romantic illusions. The truth had to come out.

"I have a confession to make, Ava."

"What?" The girl's eyes widened, as if she expected a shape-shift any second.

"Gabe and I weren't dating for real. We were faking it."

"I don't understand." Confusion in the teen's expression cut through the anger.

"It was his idea but, to be fair, I went along. He convinced me to go out, pretend to date, then break up at a mutually agreeable time."

"Why?" Ava looked completely lost.

"You had just gone rogue to Make Me a Match. I didn't know what else you might do. What drastic steps you might take. There are a lot of places out there a fourteen-year-old girl shouldn't go."

"Come on, Mom. Give me some credit."

"How was I to know? I felt the need to protect you. And his family kept trying to fix him up with different women at Sunday dinner. We thought if everyone believed we were a couple, they would stop interfering in our personal lives. It was supposed to be simple and uncomplicated. He called it an insurance policy. No one was supposed to get hurt."

"You did."

"I really like him." Courtney sighed. She was

pretty sure she was in love with him, but saying the words out loud had the potential to make this even more painful. "But the truth is that he simply doesn't want to care for someone again. He's protecting himself."

While she explained everything, the expression on Ava's face went from simmering temper to self-righteous indignation. "So what you're actually saying is that you lied."

"Yes. Wrong thing, right reason." It was a pathetic rebuttal and very likely would come back one day to bite her in the butt.

"You grounded me for half my life for lying." Ava's hostility was gaining momentum.

Courtney had no move here except to own the flaw. "You're completely right. I'm a hypocrite—"

And she started to cry again. Damn it, she'd ruined everything. There was a very good chance her daughter wanted to return her for an upgraded mother, preferably one who wasn't a fraud. And Gabe was gone. Why did he have to be so nice? He tutored high school kids in math, for crying out loud. And he was cute. He was funny and caring. A man who loved as deeply as he did was incredibly special.

"I'm sorry I made you worry, Mom. I wouldn't go anywhere on the internet I shouldn't. And I just wanted you to be happy." Ava looked at her hands and drew in a shuddering breath. "This is all my fault. If I hadn't gone to Make Me a Match, this never would have happened to you. I promise I'll never bug you to date anyone ever again. It's just you and me. Please don't cry."

With an effort, Courtney pulled herself together and brushed the tears from her cheeks. "And that is what ugly crying looks like."

"Are you okay now?" Ava looked concerned.

"I will be." She tried to smile. "On the up side, I have your solemn promise to never again meddle in my personal life. So the fake-dating scheme actually worked. Except the part where no one was supposed to get hurt—"

Now Ava started crying. "I'm so sorry, Mommy—"

She pulled the girl close and held her tight, trying to hug away the hurt she'd done. It was a disaster. Gabe couldn't love her, and this child that she'd bent over backwards to protect was hurting a lot. Now Courtney's heart was broken in two places.

Chapter Fourteen

Gabe had a bad feeling that he'd made a big mistake with Courtney the night before. And not just because he was on the way to his mom's house for Sunday dinner without her and Ava. Everyone was going to ask about them, and he'd have to talk about the breakup. This was supposed to be his glory moment, the peak of his plan, the triumph of it coming together. Why the hell didn't he feel victorious? Or at least a little better than pond scum?

He hadn't slept much last night, mostly because he couldn't get Courtney's face out of his mind. He kept seeing the shock and hurt in her expressive eyes when he said no to pursuing a real relationship. One of the things he liked best about her was that he always knew what she was feeling. And he hated himself because he was responsible for that crushed expression on her face.

But what bothered him most was the prospect of a future without Courtney in it. His life looked bleak, miserable and lonely.

All too soon he pulled the two-seater Benz to a stop in front of the house and let it idle. If there was no Courtney and Ava in his life, he wouldn't need to borrow a bigger car, or buy one. That had crossed his mind more than once. A quick vehicle count told him he was the last to arrive. Even Aunt Lil had made it. Her sensible SUV in bright red was easy to spot. The thought of leaving without going inside crossed his mind. He could make excuses later, use the breakup and not wanting to talk about it to get sympathy, which had always been the plan. After all, the more hurt they thought he was, the longer they'd give him before trying to put him back in the saddle. Just looking at all these cars made him see how many times he'd have to explain, and he realized there would be less discomfort if he took a sharp stick in the eye.

"Nope. Get it over with. One and done," he said to himself.

He shut off the car, then exited and walked up to the front door and let himself in. "Hello."

He heard his mother say, "In the family room," as if it was impossible for him to determine where the crowd noise was coming from. The entryway ended at the kitchen–family room combination, and everyone was there. Mason and Annie's twins were on the floor playing with toys while their pregnant, about-to-pop mom supervised from her position on the couch. Rumor had it she was overdue and the new baby could arrive any minute. The men, including Dominic, Mason and their dad, were holding beers and talking. They straddled both rooms.

His sister, mom and aunt Lil were in the kitchen handling food prep. When Gabe walked into view, all of them stared at him. And he could almost see their gazes look past him expectantly, as if there should be someone else.

He was going to ignore that and brazen it out, hope for the best. "Hi, all."

With dish towel in hand, his mom moved close and reached her arms up to hug him. "Hi. Where's Courtney? Did she have to work?"

"No."

"Did she have other plans?" Aunt Lil also gave him a hug.

"No."

There was something in his aunt's expression, a slice of steel and suspicion that indicated she was pretty sure he was holding something back. "So, you didn't invite her?"

"I did." Having someone know you as well as his aunt did was both a blessing and a curse. As much as he hoped the family might let this slide, deep down he'd known they wouldn't. After all, his mother was the one who'd invited Ember to dinner. Time to rip off the Band-Aid, then move on. "Courtney broke up with me."

"Why?" His sister, Kelsey, called out from the

kitchen, dashing any hope that someone, anyone, might be too busy to listen.

"It just wasn't working out." He'd rehearsed what to say, tried out different ways to phrase it so the magnitude of her being out of his life wouldn't hit him with the same crippling force. Those words were the best he could do and didn't work as intended.

"What does that mean?" His mother was frowning.

It meant she wanted more than he could give. And that he was protecting her from himself. But her words vibrated through him. *You're afraid of being hurt.* None of that would come out of his mouth in front of the three women who were staring at him now. "What does it matter? It's over."

"But she's awesome, Gabe." Dom, his bachelor brother, called out from the male group, who were obviously listening.

"It's just one of those things. I could use a beer," he said.

Aunt Lil took a step to the side and blocked his path to the refrigerator. "I can see by the look on your face there's more to this. I'd like to know what really happened between you and Courtney."

"I told you." All his life this woman had looked at him with love and patient indulgence. She'd never glared as if he was frightening children or deliberately crushing flowers under his heel. But she was now. Disappointing her put him on defense, big-time. "She's terrific, but I'm not good enough for her."

"Did she say that?" Aunt Lil demanded. "Because

I'm a pretty good judge of character, and that doesn't sound like something Courtney would say."

"She didn't exactly say that," he admitted. Although it was definitely true. He was another jerk who'd let her down, and that thought made him want to put his fist through a wall. And true to form, he was using anger to handle loss.

"You might be able to sell this ridiculous story to someone who doesn't know you well, but for me it doesn't pass the smell test. Don't interrupt me." Aunt Lil put up a hand to stop him when he opened his mouth to say something. "After Margo died, you were furious and had every right to be. I get it. Anyone who's lost someone they love understands the rage you feel at the overwhelming grief and loneliness. I felt exactly the same when your uncle Phil died. Anger is one of the stages of grief, and he was the love of my life."

Gabe wasn't sure where she was going with this and didn't really want to know. Wherever it was, he wasn't going to like it. "And you found a way to channel your feelings, Aunt Lil. You bought Make Me a Match, and bringing people together is healing you—"

"We're talking about you, Gabriel," she said sternly. "I understand why a grief-stricken person holds on to their anger. In some twisted way, it keeps that loved one alive, at the same time squeezing out the heartache and pain."

"Makes sense," he said. "Thanks for sharing."

"Not so fast." She looked pretty fierce now. "You

carried that anger for a long time. But after meeting Courtney, it disappeared. I see it again today, and I believe that's because you really care about her. And you lost her."

"No, I—"

"Death is permanent," she continued as if he hadn't spoken. "But you're still on this earth, and so is Courtney. Whatever happened, there's still time for you to fix it."

He couldn't deny that she was right about him being angry, and the more she pushed and backed him into a corner, the hotter he got. This felt like death by a thousand cuts, and he wanted it over. There was only one way to do that.

"Courtney and I were never serious." As soon as the statement came out of his mouth, he felt the untruth in it. But the red haze of anger didn't leave room for reasonable thought to shut him up. "We were fake dating."

"You were what now?" His father looked clueless.

"We were going out so that her daughter and my family—" he pointed to each of them "—that would be all of you, would cease and desist interfering in our lives and pushing us to find someone. Ava came to Make Me a Match, but she could easily have ended up somewhere dangerous for a young girl. Courtney was desperate to find a way to get her to stop."

"And you?" His mother had let her sister take the lead on this interrogation, but the reprieve was over. And her voice was like ice.

"Every Sunday there was another woman here,

an obvious attempt to hook me up. Has anyone ever told you you're not subtle? And you have to admit that was interfering in my life."

"Well, excuse us for caring." His mom looked close to tears.

"Pardon us for hoping you would move on with your life and find happiness." Aunt Lil's tone was identical to her sister's.

"Yeah. We were just trying to help." Mason had been quiet up until now, but he'd obviously been listening. "You're on your own now, brother. When you end up a lonely, bitter old man, you'll have no one to blame but yourself."

"I'm sorry," Gabe said. "But that last dinner with Ember pushed me over the edge."

"Understood," his mother snapped. "That was all on me, and never fear. It won't happen again."

God, he hated his mother's angry, hurt voice. "Look, Mom—"

She brushed a hand over her cheek and turned away, probably to hide the tears in her eyes. "Dinner's almost ready. You should get that beer."

"So I'm not in time-out?" He was trying to lighten the moment, but no one cracked a smile. "Okay. I'll get a beer."

"Suit yourself." Aunt Lil followed his mother to the kitchen.

The men went back to talking sports while the women were putting final touches on the food. The truth was out, and the world was still spinning. Gabe should have felt relieved that everything was now out in the open. His family was clearly upset, but he figured they'd get over this breakup with Courtney. But would he?

After snagging a beer from the fridge, he went into the family room, where Charlie and Sarah were busily playing with plastic containers and wooden spoons from their grandmother's kitchen. Maybe the two toddlers were still speaking to him.

Charlie tottered over like a drunken sailor and handed him a plastic leftover container lid. There was a question in his blue eyes, then he looked around at all the grown-ups present. Apparently he didn't see the person he had expected to. "Awa?"

Then little Sarah was in front of him asking, "Awa? Hewe?"

He looked at their mother for translation. "What did they just say?"

Annie sighed as she rubbed her big belly. "When they've seen you recently, Courtney and Ava were with you. They want to know where Ava is. They really like her."

"Oh." In their own way, even these babies were smacking him upside the head. "You can sure tell they're Blackburnes. As if I haven't already replaced the lowest life form on the planet, they're making me feel worse than slime."

"Fake dating, huh?" Annie shook her head. "That was a pretty radical plan."

He'd wanted them off his back and now they

were, but he hadn't anticipated this. Because no one was ever supposed to find out about the plot. Still, he would go down defending his actions until hell wouldn't have it. "Desperate times call for desperate measures. Those people were out of control."

"Try and cut them some slack." She tucked a strand of blond hair behind her ear. "Everything they did was out of love."

"Love, huh? Maybe I could do with a little less of it."

"You don't mean that, Gabe." Annie's expression was sympathetic, but there was an edge in it, too. Reproach. "Take it from me. You can never have too much love."

"And take it from me, I was up to here with their butting in."

She shrugged as if to say, "Agree to disagree," and they sat quietly, watching the kids.

Activity went on around him for the rest of the day. Eventually the family actually spoke to him as if he wasn't public enemy number one. But his sister-in-law's words echoed in his head.

They did everything out of love.

Had he done that with Courtney? Believing he would hurt her, had he shut the door on anything more with her? Funny how much bigger his loneliness was after knowing her, being with her. And the way he missed her wasn't fake. The need to hold her wasn't a sham. The feelings had been growing, but he told himself they weren't real. They weren't love.

He'd been so wrong about that.

* * *

After a moping-over-Gabe day, which was only interrupted by eating ice cream, Courtney had never been so happy to be at work. Productive activity was the best antidote to heartache and took her mind off missing him so deeply. Unfortunately, work didn't always cooperate with her objectives. Her lady with the broken heart had been discharged with orders to see her primary care physician for ongoing treatment. And, happily, there were only a couple of patients in the unit for observation, none of them terribly sick.

For once she had time to stay current with patient charting and was at the nurses' station doing just that. But it was taking longer than usual because thoughts of Gabe kept popping into her mind to torture her. The trip to the zoo where he delighted Ava with a stuffed giraffe. He'd been so kind and understanding when her daughter showed up at his office to find her pathetic mother a man. So sweet and supportive when she'd lost such a young patient. If only his kisses hadn't absolutely melted her into a puddle of liquid lust.

Would this be any easier if he weren't quite so good-looking? A little less sexy? She thought not, because the things that made him so special were on the inside, his heart and soul. His integrity.

His biggest flaw was one of character, something that made it impossible for her to be mad at him. He couldn't forgive himself for not fulfilling the wish of the woman he had loved. He wouldn't let himself see that what had happened was a tragic twist of fate, not a failure on his part. He hadn't committed a crime. Ironically, he'd just wanted more time to secure their future, and he would have done things differently if he could have seen into the future. He might have had a child now and known the joy of parenting, even if he had to do it alone.

Courtney could see into her future, and it was fairly empty. Ava *would* be going to college in a few years, leaving her mom behind. It was a lonely prospect, made even lonelier because she'd had a glimpse of how it might look with the right man. And Gabe was the right one for her. She was absolutely convinced of that.

"Are you going to stare into space a little longer or get that charting done?" The voice belonged to Sharon Ridley.

Courtney jumped. She'd been so lost in her thoughts, she hadn't seen her supervisor walk into the nurses' station. The woman was fiftyish with dark hair cut pixie short.

"Sorry, Sharon. No excuses. My brain was hijacked by aliens."

"It happens. Anything you want to talk about?"

"No. Maybe another time. But thanks," Courtney said.

"On the plus side, you've got the time for contemplation since we're not swamped with patients." This woman had a great management style and seamlessly navigated the gray area between boss and friend. "That's fortunate."

Not really. Courtney would have preferred being too busy to think. "A breather is always good."

"Why don't you take your lunch now?" Sharon suggested. "It would actually be on time for a change. That almost never happens."

"Okay. I'll just finish up this charting." She shrugged. "This time I will really do it."

"I never doubted it. Have a good lunch."

"Thanks for understanding." Courtney sincerely meant that.

About fifteen minutes later, she left the nurses' station and walked down the corridor to the fourth-floor elevators. She managed to get one that was empty and pushed the down button. With a sigh, she leaned against the wall and wondered why she was exhausted when there was less work to do. On the third floor, the doors whispered open to let someone on.

And Florence Blackburne, Gabriel's mother, was that someone.

They stared at each other for so long the automatic elevator doors started to close. Courtney stuck out her arm to stop them from shutting in the other woman's face.

"Thanks." She smiled a little sadly. "Hi, Courtney."

"Mrs. Blackburne. How are you?" Then she remembered that she worked where sick people go for help. That gave her stomach a lurch. "Is everyone okay?"

"Yes. Why? Oh—this is a hospital." Flo nodded

her understanding. "Annie's in labor. Finally. She was sure this baby was never going to get here."

"That's wonderful."

"We're very excited. John and Lillian are here. We're so happy to have some good news in the family."

Bull's-eye, Courtney thought. Of course Gabe would tell his mother they'd "broken up." Fortunately the elevator doors opened then and she could escape.

She stepped out and looked at the other woman. "I'm on my way to lunch. Give Annie my best. Sorry things with Gabe and I didn't go well—" Without warning, a lump of emotion caught in her throat, and she stopped. Of all the times to get weepy, in front of Florence Blackburne would not have been her first choice.

"Courtney—" The woman got out, took her by the arm and led her to a quiet hallway just around the corner from the elevators. "What is it?"

"Oh—" She waved her hand dismissively and sniffled. "Babies and breakups do it to me every time."

"Hmm. So you're upset about what happened between you and my son?"

There was nothing to be gained by not telling the truth. This had been the objective from the beginning—to convince the pertinent parties that they were a thing, then be sad when it was over. And what a relief not to feel like a double agent anymore. Except that she was really hurting, and her mouth trembled when she nodded and more tears filled her eyes.

"I love my son, so don't take this the wrong way. But Gabriel is a bonehead."

"Wh-what?"

"Courtney, I know you're on your lunch break, but would you do me a favor and come up to the maternity waiting room with me? I promise not to keep you too long."

Face the Blackburnes? There was a knot in her stomach the size of an MRI machine, and that would make eating lunch a challenge. Call it balancing out yesterday's ice cream binge. "I don't know—"

"Please, honey. They'd all like to see you. Honestly."

The woman's sincerity reminded Courtney of Flo's son and his integrity. She allowed herself to trust that this wasn't an ambush. "Okay."

So the two of them went back around the corner and into the first up elevator that came. They rode it to the third floor, where maternity was located. And there in the waiting room were Gabe's father and his aunt Lillian. The two of them stood when they saw Courtney.

Flo urged her forward and chattered nonstop. "Mason is in the labor room with Annie. Kelsey is working today and will pop in when she can. Dom and Gabe are at work now. They're coming later."

Courtney wondered if she would feel it when he walked into the building. Like a disturbance in the force. Hopefully she wouldn't see him and have yet another place with memories of him that she had to proactively forget. This woman was remarkably chipper. And friendly.

"Look who I found in the elevator," Flo said when they stopped in front of the other two.

"Hi." Courtney lifted a hand in greeting, wondering whether or not she should be freaked out by the friendliness. If this was a horror movie—and it was beginning to have that feeling—right about now they would turn on her.

But Gabe's mother jumped right in to fill the silence. "This young woman could use some cheering up. She's feeling sad about the way things with Gabriel turned out."

Looking confused, her husband scratched his head. "But I thought that was all fake. So you would stop throwing women at him, Florence."

"Oh, John—" His wife gave him that affectionate, indulgent look that women do when their man has no clue about the obvious emotional undercurrents going on around him.

But Courtney wasn't fortunate enough to be oblivious. She realized exactly what was going on. "You guys know?"

"He told us when you didn't come to dinner on Sunday," Lillian explained.

"I can't believe you're even speaking to me," she said. "I'm completely ashamed about trying to deceive you all. My only excuse is that I was worried about Ava."

"He told us. And that it was all his idea." Lillian's gaze took on a shrewd gleam. "But, unless I miss my guess, the two of you got something more than you, literally, bargained for."

"Not him," Courtney hurried to explain. "Just me. I mentioned the idea of dating for real, but he said no."

"Blockhead," his mother muttered.

"No. He's a really good man. Like his father, I'd guess." She smiled sadly at the man who'd been such a good role model to his son. "I appreciate his honesty. A lot of men would have taken advantage of the situation, but he didn't. He's really quite wonderful—" She swallowed the emotions that crept up on her.

"Oh, honey—" Flo slid an arm around her waist and pulled her close.

"It's going to be all right. You'll see." Lillian moved to her other side and put her arm around her, too.

Courtney held back a sob. She'd never in her life felt support like this. When her parents found out she was going to be a teenage mother, her family had fallen apart. How she would have cherished being a part of this one. But it wasn't meant to be. And, while she appreciated Lillian's words, she just didn't see how anything was going to be all right ever again.

"Thank you all for understanding." Courtney looked at each of them in turn, willing them to know how sorry she was. "And I truly regret trying to fake you out."

"That doesn't matter. The important thing is that you and Gabriel found each other. Without my help,

I'm sad to say." Lillian took her hands. "But if you don't believe anything else, believe this. There's nothing phony about the way you looked at my nephew. Or the way he looked at you."

"That's what I thought, too. But I was wrong." Courtney shrugged.

"I don't take you for a quitter," Lillian said firmly. "Don't you give up on him, young lady."

She wasn't the one who gave up. He'd quit on her before they even tried to see if it could work.

Courtney hugged each of them, then walked away. There was a crushing weight on her chest. In a perfect world, this family could have been hers. But it wasn't and never could be. Because Gabe wasn't hers and never would be. Without him, her world could never be complete. How could it be when she'd given him her heart?

Chapter Fifteen

Gabe was at the high school waiting for Ava to show up for her tutoring session, although he wasn't at all sure she would come. After all, she probably knew about the breakup. But he hadn't been able to confirm that for sure, since Courtney wasn't answering his calls. He missed that woman with everything he had. And it had only been a couple of days since he'd last seen her. Length of time wasn't the issue. It was the thought of never seeing her again that had him feeling a little on the desperate side.

Courtney had become so very important to him, and now he felt lost. Shutting her out, closing himself off from feelings for her might just be the biggest mistake he'd ever made. For crying out loud, he fixed financially ailing companies for a living, but he couldn't fix his own life. Now he realized that without her, he had no life. He was going to make her see that or die trying.

But first he needed to honor his commitment to Ava, to making sure she passed her math test. He had to admit that he'd missed the kid, too. And now he was pacing, nervous and impatient for her to show up, making another circuit of the classroom that seemed too small all of a sudden. His cell phone vibrated, and it was a welcome distraction.

He fished it out of his pocket and checked the caller ID, hoping it was Courtney. It wasn't. His mom's name and number came up, and he swiped the green button. "Hi, Mom. What's going on?"

"You wanted updates on Annie. This is it."

"How is she?"

His mother sighed, and it sounded a lot like helpless frustration. "Not much change. It's going very slowly. I feel so badly for her. Mason is holding it together for her sake, but it's hard to watch someone you love hurting, even when there's going to be a good outcome. But she's hanging in there like the trouper she is."

"Where are the twins?" he asked.

"Labor started in the middle of the night, so Mason's next-door neighbor came over to watch them. Dad and I wanted to be here at the hospital for him and Annie. Your dad just left to go get the twins and bring them to be with us. They can play with toys and run around the waiting room. There are enough of us to take care of them. That's about it for now. I wish I had something more to report."

"Okay, Mom. Thanks for the update."

"When are you coming over?"

"In a little while. Carla is holding down the fort at Make Me a Match."

"So what are you doing now?" she asked.

"Math tutoring."

"Is it your day to do that?"

"One of the students made special arrangements."

"Okay," she said. "See you when you get here. If there's any news before that, I'll let you know."

"Thanks. 'Bye." As he hung up, a noise in the classroom doorway made him turn. Ava was standing there, backpack slung over her shoulder.

There was surprise on her face, but almost instantly it changed to open hostility and a whole lot of resentment. "I'm not staying. Just checking. I didn't think you'd be here."

"Why wouldn't I?" Of course he knew, but he wanted to keep her talking. He needed to find out what information she had about Courtney. It was essential to protect the secret and not say anything about their agreement. His family had reacted badly, and they were adults. An impressionable fourteen-year-old girl could be a lot worse.

"Well, you're not dating my mother anymore, for one thing."

He winced at the lethal emphasis on the D-word and had a feeling the secret was no longer classified. "You know."

"That you were pretending to like my mom?" The heated look in her eyes could laser paint off the wall. "Yeah, I know."

"I wasn't pretending to like her. And when I give my word, I don't break it. So let's do some algebra."

"Do you think I'm stupid? I already did the math, and this is the answer I got. You're just like all the other jerks. And I thought you were going to be different." Disillusionment put a dimmer switch on the shine in her eyes until it flickered and went out.

"Like all the others?" he asked.

"Guys who say what they think you want to hear just to get what they want."

"I wouldn't do that," Gabe protested. "Like I said, when I give my word, you can count on me to keep it."

"Why should I believe you? You lied to me and to your family. My mom told me why she went along with it, and I promised not to bug her anymore, but the lie was all your idea. How would you even think of something like that? Unless lies are second nature to you. Just like all men."

"Ava, no. I admit that wasn't my finest hour, but my family—" He dragged his fingers through his hair. "The last woman they set me up with at Sunday dinner was named Ember. Do *that* math."

"So?" But for a second her mouth softened into an almost smile. "Ember? Really?"

"It was vital that I make them stop." He shrugged. "The way I chose to do that was wrong."

"Do they know?"

"Yes." If ever there was a time for complete transparency, this was it. So he added, "I didn't plan to tell them."

"Like I said, you'll say, or not say, anything to get what you want."

If he was a bug, there would be a stain on the bottom of her white canvas shoe about now. "I'm not a bad guy. You have to trust me."

"Really?" There was an edge of shrillness in her voice. "You mean the way I could trust the sperm donor who got my mom pregnant then ran out on her and me? Before I was even born."

"Ava, listen—"

"No." The backpack must have been heavy, because she slid it off her shoulder and let it rest on a desk. "Maybe you think I should trust you like the jackass who convinced my mom he loved her and me. He claimed he wanted to be a real dad to me. And I really wanted one. Mom believed the lie because she wanted me to have a family like she never had. And she went right on believing until after she married him and right away he started talking about having *real* kids."

"That's not me—"

"Well, you know what?" She glared at him, highlighting the fury and pain inside her. "I am a real kid. I have real feelings, and he took advantage of that to make promises and fool me. You did the same thing, and I hate that I fell for it again. I'm so stupid—"

"You're not. It wasn't supposed to happen like this, and I hate that it did. I'm really sorry."

"Why should I believe you? The idea to lie was yours." She shook her head. "My mom is right. You can't trust men."

He was seeing the destruction of this girl's romantic streak, which was exactly what Courtney had tried to prevent. He hated himself for many things, but never more than doing this to an innocent girl's illusions. "I'm a jerk. A real piece of work."

"Wow, the truth," she said sarcastically. "I'd have called you a jackass. And here's why. You don't care about my mom at all, and you never did."

"You're wrong about that, Ava. I liked your mother the first time I met her, right here at your school. She's beautiful and smart and funny. She touched my heart right away, and that scared me, but it was okay. Because I never expected to see her again. And I was glad about that."

"Why?" There was still resentment, buckets of it, but at least she was listening to him.

"I never wanted to care about a woman again."

"Because your wife died. Mom told me about that."

"Yes. And I never wanted to put myself in a position to feel pain and loss like that again. Being alone was better. Until I met your mother. Then you came in to Make Me a Match to find her a man, and your plan worked. I didn't know it right then, but I was a goner."

Ava caught her top lip between her teeth. For the first time since walking through the classroom door, she looked uncertain. There was a crack in her antagonism. "Do you really think I'm stupid enough to believe you?" She pointed at him. "And before you answer that, remember I was grounded for a really long time for telling my mom that I was somewhere I wasn't."

Gabe blew out a long breath. "There's absolutely no reason for you to believe me, but this is the honest truth. Until I came up with the fake-dating plan, I didn't lie. Except the time my sister asked me if her jeans made her butt look big. And I was kidding to get a reaction from her."

That got a reluctant smile. "I don't know—"

"Telling lies doesn't come naturally to me." It was really important to him to win back Ava's trust. Not just because he truly cared about her. But without her in his corner, there was no way for him to win back her mother. "I'll prove to you that I'm telling the truth if we can relocate this tutoring session to the hospital."

"But Mom's working," she protested.

"I know." Before he became public jackass number one, Courtney had given him her schedule for the month. "If she's busy, I won't bother her until she's off work. But there's another reason."

"What?" Ava asked suspiciously.

"Annie's gone into labor."

"She's having the baby?" The teen's eyes went wide with excitement.

"Yes. The whole family is gathering, and I'd like to be there with them when the baby gets here." And he hoped this would be the icing on his apology cake. "My dad is bringing Sarah and Charlie over."

"I would like to see the twins." She was fighting it but weakening.

"I have to talk to your mom and apologize," he said firmly.

"Good plan. I like it." She nodded her approval. "Can I watch?"

"No." But he grinned.

"Okay. I'm in. Mom won't mind if I don't take the bus home. Wrong thing, right reason. She's all about me passing my math test. So tutoring at the hospital, it is. Do you have the Mercedes? Or are you driving your dad's boring SUV?"

"Nope, it's the Benz." He grinned. "And I seem to recall promising you a ride in it."

She smiled. The Ava who liked him was back. "You really do keep your promises."

"It's kind of my thing."

"Let's go, then," she said.

One Davidson down. Now it was time for him to plead his case to the other one—the woman who'd stolen his heart against his will.

After talking to Gabe's family, Courtney was a little distracted for the rest of the day. Their words kept floating through her mind. *You're not a quitter. Don't give up on him.* They'd been so gracious about her deception, she'd nearly broken down and sobbed in front of them. They seemed to genuinely like her and to be sincerely thankful she and Gabe had found each other. But she was the only one who'd found what she wanted, and being the only one made her heart hurt. Unfortunately, there was no medication or therapy on the planet that would cure what she had.

On top of that, he was coming to the hospital because of the new baby. Was he here now? Would she have sensed it if he was in the building? She was exhausted from thinking about it. Thank goodness her shift was done. It was time to go home, where Ava was waiting for her. That was the good news. The bad was that she would never get over Gabriel, but she'd learn to live without him. It might take some time, but survivor was her middle name. She wouldn't always have her daughter to lean on, but she would make the most of it while she could.

"Hey, Courtney. I didn't see you at lunch." Taylor came out of the elevator and met her at the nurses' station. "You heading home?"

"Yeah." And nothing to look forward to there. Except Ava, of course. But not Gabe. Never again him. And that sad thought left a mark.

"Any plans?"

She hadn't had a chance to clue in her friend about recent developments. "No plans."

"What's wrong? Problems with your guy?"

"He isn't my guy and never has been." Courtney didn't want to air her personal problems right there by the nurse's station and moved her friend away, to the other side of the hall by the elevator.

"Do you want to talk about it?"

The elevator doors beside them opened just then,

and a guy got out. Courtney looked closer, and when she recognized the man, her heart skipped a beat, then started to pound. "Gabriel."

"Courtney, I—" He stopped and looked at her friend. "Sorry to interrupt."

"Gabe, this is Taylor. She works in the neonatal intensive care unit here at the hospital."

"Nice to meet you." He shook her hand.

"I've heard a lot about you." Her friend was giving him a thorough appraisal.

"She's my BFF," Courtney said, but her cheeks were burning when she looked at him. "I'm on my way home."

There were shadows in his eyes, and he looked tired. "Can I talk to you for a minute?"

"I was just leaving." There was a gleam in Taylor's eyes. A look that said she wanted a full report later. "See you tomorrow, Court. Nice to meet you, Gabe." The elevator doors opened just then, and Taylor got in before wiggling her fingers in a farewell gesture.

Gabe stared at the closed doors for several moments, then at her. "Hi, Courtney."

"Why are you here?"

"I wanted to let you know that Annie had her baby."

"That's great." She waited for more. "And? Boy or girl? How much did he/she weigh? How are they doing?"

"Right. Details that men always forget." He smiled, but it didn't break through the shadows still in his eyes. "It's a girl weighing eight pounds, four ounces. Mother, daughter, father and siblings are in seventh heaven."

"That's wonderful news. Congratulations. I saw your mom, dad and aunt Lillian earlier, so I knew she was in labor. Thanks for letting me know. I have to go now—"

"The whole family is here peeking at her in the newborn nursery. Ava is with them. I hope it's okay, but we moved our math tutoring session here to the hospital to be on baby watch."

"She's supposed to take the bus home. If there are any changes of plan, she knows she has to call me and get an okay." Then a thought sneaked in. "Oh no—she didn't come to your office again—"

"No. Nothing like that." He took a step closer. "Like I said, I was at school for a tutoring session. I hope it's okay that I brought her here. She wanted to see Charlie and Sarah and the new baby."

"It's fine." She knew Ava was fine with him and somehow he'd won back her daughter's trust. "So you did show up. She didn't think you would." Courtney hadn't been sure, either.

"Of course I did. I gave my word. And I'm a little irritated that there was any doubt. What is it with you two?"

"We've been let down before," she said quietly.

Seeing him again was killing her. It was killing her *not* to see him, too, but being this close, feeling the warmth of his body and seeing the concern in his eyes, brought a fresh wave of pain. "I appreciate you helping her. And I'm sure she loved seeing the twins and the new baby. But I have to go. I'll text her to meet me at the car—"

"Wait, Courtney. I need to talk to you."

"Why? You already said everything there was to say. That no was pretty clear. What more could you possibly want with me? Why aren't you with your family?"

"I already said hello to the baby." He looked down for a moment, and when he met her gaze again, his eyes blazed with intensity. "But right now I'm having a heart problem, and I came to you to get it fixed."

"I don't believe you." Correction: she didn't *want* to believe him. It would hurt too much to hope for a different answer and be wrong.

"I understand why you feel that way. But I promise I'm going to prove it to you. You're the only one who can help me."

"Since when do you need help? You've got all the bases covered. The man with a plan."

"Yeah, I thought I had things all figured out," he admitted. "Then I met you. Men plan and God laughs. This whole time, since coming home to Huntington Hills, I've been going on about getting Make Me a Match fixed because I wanted to move ahead with my next step. This whole time, my act two was right in front of me, and I was too stupid to get it."

"I have no idea what you mean." *Liar, liar, pants on fire.* She knew hope could be cruel and wanted no part of being made a fool of again.

"*You* were right in front of me."

"But you said you cared about me too much to hurt me," she reminded him.

He looked down and sighed. "Yeah, I deserve that. And you said I was afraid of being hurt again and hiding from life's possibilities to protect myself."

"And you told me I was hiding behind motherhood to protect myself." He wasn't wrong. That's why the fake-dating thing had seemed like the perfect plan for both of them. "So we were hiding together in plain sight."

"Courtney, I wish I could take all of that back. I was an idiot. When you talked about dating for real, you caught me off guard, and that response was knee jerk." He took her hands and wouldn't let go when she tried to pull away. "Let me make this clear. You're the only one who can fix my heart, because I'm in love with you."

"Oh—" Her voice was breathless, and with every hope and dream she'd ever had, she prayed that this was for real. "And you know this—how?"

"I knew it when you told me to leave. Everything inside me was saying that if I left you, it was the worst mistake of my life."

"But you did it anyway."

"And confirmed that it *was* the worst mistake I've ever made. Please let me make it right." He looked so sincere. "If there's one thing I do well, it's fixing things."

"Ava was pretty mad at you. I had to tell her about the fake dating to get you out of the doghouse even a little."

"Yeah, she mentioned that." He blew out a breath. "We talked, and she told me she'd never believe anything a guy says to her. I hated that. If it's the last thing I ever do, I will prove that she can trust me, Courtney. The thing is, I love her, too. You two are a package deal. A family. More than anything, I want to be part of it. I'm a guy who wants to be a dad, and she's a kid who might need one."

Courtney's eyes filled with tears. "She forgave you?"

"I took her for a ride in the Benz. And I promised to grovel when I talked to you. She liked that plan a lot more than I was comfortable with." He searched her face, waiting. "I sure wish you'd say something. If not, I can keep up the groveling—"

"No." She threw herself into his arms. "I'm in love with you, too."

"Thank God." He hugged her close, as if he'd never let go. "And I have another deal for you."

She moved back, not out of his arms but just enough to see his face. Being held like this was the absolute best feeling in the whole world. "What do you have in mind?"

"How about we date? For real. After an appropriate amount of time has gone by, I will go down on one knee and, with a very expensive diamond ring, I will ask you to marry me."

"I think I like that idea very much." She grinned up at him. "And after an appropriate amount of time passes and you go down on one knee holding a lovely and tasteful ring and request my hand in marriage, I will say yes."

"Should we shake on it?" He didn't make a move to let her go.

"No. Let's kiss on it. Just like in those romantic cartoons Ava watches."

"Excellent suggestion." He cupped her face in his hands and touched his mouth to hers.

There was nothing fake about this kiss. Or the love that had sneaked up on both of them when they weren't looking. This time it was for real.

Epilogue

Six months later

"Mom, don't you have something nicer to wear?"

Courtney glanced down at her most worn and comfortable jeans and the giraffe T-shirt Gabe had bought her at their recent trip to the zoo with Ava. "What's wrong with this?"

Ava gave her clothes a supercritical once-over. "Mr. B is coming for dinner. I just thought you'd want to look nice."

"I think I look nice. Besides, it's just clothes." And Gabe liked these jeans, especially taking them off.

"But, Mom—" It looked as if Ava was about to explode with frustration. "You have those new slacks. And the sweater that looks so amazing on you."

Courtney finished cutting up cucumbers and put them in the green salad along with shredded carrots. "This is comfortable, just like the meat loaf we're having tonight. We're only hanging out and watching movies."

"But what if you're not? What if—" Ava stopped talking, and her eyes went wide.

"Ava?" She put a hand on her hip and studied her daughter. "What aren't you telling me?"

"Nothing. I tell you everything, Mom." The look on her teenager's face was too angelic to be believed.

Courtney didn't buy into it for a second. "Come clean, kiddo. Something's going on. And it's Saturday night. You almost always get together with your friends. Why are you voluntarily staying home to be with the grown-ups?"

Her daughter moved in for a hug. "Because I love you."

"Aw. I love you, too." She stepped back and tucked long strands of Ava's silky hair behind her ears. "And I know you better than anyone. So, tell me—"

The doorbell rang, and Ava was super excited when she said, "Mr. B is here."

Just before she sprinted away to let him in, Courtney was sure she heard her daughter say, "Thank God." It was several moments of whispering before Gabe walked into her kitchen with what looked like a dozen red roses and a mysterious smile.

"Hi." He moved closer and slid his arm around her waist to bring her against him, then lowered his mouth to hers.

The kiss was more tender than usual and filled with a promise that left her breathless. "Hi, yourself."

He took her hand and led her around the corner and into the living room, where Ava was sitting on the couch. Her eyes were dancing with excitement.

Gabe sat her down beside her daughter. "I'd like to talk to you about something."

"Okay." She glanced at her teenager. "Do you know anything about this?"

"Just be patient, Mom. All will be revealed." But she was practically quivering with anticipation.

Gabe sat on the leather ottoman in front of them and handed Ava six roses from the bouquet before giving Courtney the other half dozen. "Flowers for my two favorite ladies."

"Thanks, Mr. B. No one ever gave me flowers before." Ava seemed surprised but pleased by the gesture.

"They're beautiful, Gabe." Courtney breathed in the sweet, fresh floral scent. "I love them. I need to put them in some water—"

"Wait. There's more." He took a small jewelry box from his jeans pocket and went down on one knee before opening it. A stunning diamond ring sparkled against the black velvet background. He looked at Ava. "Okay, kid, we talked about this. Speak now or forever hold your peace. I want to make sure it's okay with you if I marry your mom."

"Totally okay." She nodded enthusiastically.

Courtney had truly never seen her child so happy. "You discussed this?"

"I helped him pick out the ring," Ava said proudly. "It's called an Open Arms engagement ring. The setting interlocks with the three diamonds."

"They represent the three of us," Gabe explained. "As well as the past, present and future. The past made us who we are. The present and future includes the three of us together."

The thoughtfulness and beauty of the ring and this moment brought tears to Courtney's eyes. Now the clothes critique made sense.

She looked at Ava. "So, you were in on this."

"Yes." She beamed at Gabe and nodded. "I'm cool with it."

"Okay, then." He met Courtney's gaze, and his own was filled with undisguised love. "An appropriate amount of time has passed, and my feelings for you have only grown deeper and stronger. Courtney, I love you with all my heart. Will you marry me and make me the happiest man on the planet?"

"Yes—" Emotion formed a lump in her throat, and that one word was all she could squeeze past it. But it was the most important one, the one she'd promised to say that day in the hospital.

He lifted the ring from its black velvet nest and took her left hand to slide it onto the proper finger. "A perfect fit, thanks to Ava."

"You're welcome." Ava looked from him to her mother. "Now hurry up and make it official so he can move in here with us. I know that's why you're waiting, even though I'm aware that people do actually live together before they get married."

"Anything else?" Courtney asked wryly.

"As a matter of fact—" There was an earnest expression on her daughter's face. "You two need to think about having kids. Don't get me wrong—I'm happy to be getting a math tutor and a dad. Call me greedy, but I'd like a real brother or sister."

"Wow—" Courtney couldn't stop the happy tears that trickled down her cheeks. She pulled Ava into a hug. "Thank you, sweetie. I love you to the moon and back."

"I love you more." Ava sniffled and said, "But aren't you supposed to tell him that? And a kiss would be good, too. It's what they always do at the end of the cartoon romances."

"You're right." She handed Ava her flowers to hold, then slid forward and put her arms around Gabe's neck. "I love you to the moon and stars and beyond."

"I love you more." He kissed her and then said, "That's to seal the deal. No backing out now."

"As if… How could I when I'm so grateful we met?"

"You're welcome again," Ava said. "I think you owe me a grounding credit."

"When you're a little older, there's a job waiting for you at Make Me a Match." Gabe grinned at her. "But for now, would you mind putting your mom's flowers in water?"

"You got it, Mr. B—I mean, Dad."

Ava said it shyly, as if testing out the word. But what a beautiful start. When they were alone, Courtney kissed him. "And that's so you can't back out."

"Not a chance. You and Ava are the family I never thought I'd have. I wouldn't trade this for anything."

"Me either. This time it's for real."

* * * * *

Don't miss the next book by Teresa Southwick,
The Cowboy's Promise,
the fourth book in the Montana Mavericks:
What Happened to Beatrix? continuity,
available in October 2020 from
Harlequin Special Edition!

WE HOPE YOU ENJOYED
THIS BOOK FROM

HARLEQUIN
SPECIAL
EDITION

Believe in love. Overcome obstacles. Find happiness.

Relate to finding comfort and strength in the
support of loved ones and enjoy the journey
no matter what life throws your way.

6 NEW BOOKS AVAILABLE EVERY MONTH!

HSEHALO2020

COMING NEXT MONTH FROM

H HARLEQUIN

SPECIAL EDITION

Available August 18, 2020

#2785 THE MAVERICK'S BABY ARRANGEMENT
Montana Mavericks: What Happened to Beatrix?
by Kathy Douglass
In order to retain custody of his eight-month-old niece, Daniel Dubois convinces event planner and confirmed businesswoman Brittany Brandt to marry him. It's only supposed to be a mutually beneficial business agreement...*if* they can both keep their hearts out of the equation.

#2786 THE LAST MAN SHE EXPECTED
Welcome to Starlight • by Michelle Major
When Mara Reed agrees to partner with her sworn enemy, Parker Johnson, to help a close friend, she doesn't expect the feelings of love and tenderness that complicate every interaction with the handsome attorney. Will Mara and Parker risk everything for love?

#2787 CHANGING HIS PLANS
Gallant Lake Stories • by Jo McNally
Real estate developer Brittany Doyle is eager to bring the mountain town of Gallant Lake into the twenty-first century...by changing everything. Hardware store owner Nate Thomas hates change. These opposites refuse to compromise, except when it comes to falling in love.

#2788 A WINNING SEASON
Wickham Falls Weddings • by Rochelle Alers
When Sutton Reed returns to Wickham Falls after finishing a successful baseball career, he assumes he'll just join the family business and live an uneventful life. Until his neighbor's younger brother tries to steal his car, that is. Now he's finding himself mentoring the boy—and being drawn to Zoey Allen like no one else.

#2789 IN SERVICE OF LOVE
Sutter Creek, Montana • by Laurel Greer
Commitmentphobic veterinarian Maggie is focused on training a Great Dane as a service dog and expanding the family dog-training business. Can widowed single dad Asher's belief in love after loss inspire Maggie to risk her heart and find forever with the irresistible librarian?

#2790 THE SLOW BURN
Masterson, Texas • by Caro Carson
When firefighter Caden Sterling unexpectedly delivers Tana McKenna's baby by the side of the road, the unlikely threesome forms a special bond. Their flirty friendship slowly becomes more, until Tana's ex and the truth about her baby catches up with her. Can she win back the only man who can make this family complete?

YOU CAN FIND MORE INFORMATION ON UPCOMING HARLEQUIN TITLES, FREE EXCERPTS AND MORE AT HARLEQUIN.COM.

HSECNM0820

SPECIAL EXCERPT FROM

H HARLEQUIN
SPECIAL EDITION

*Real estate developer Brittany Doyle is eager to
bring the mountain town of Gallant Lake into the
twenty-first century...by changing everything.
Hardware store owner Nate Thomas hates change.
These opposites refuse to compromise, except when it
comes to falling in love.*

Read on for a sneak peek at
Changing His Plans,
*the next book in the Gallant Lake Stories
miniseries by Jo McNally.*

He stuck his head around the corner of the fasteners
aisle just in time to see a tall brunette stagger into the
revolving seed display. Some of the packets went flying,
but she managed to steady the display before the whole
thing toppled. He took in what probably had been a very
nice silk blouse and tailored trouser suit before she was
drenched in the storm raging outside. The heel on one of
the ridiculously high heels she was wearing had snapped
off, explaining why she was stumbling around.

"Having a bad morning?"

The woman looked up in annoyance, strands of dark,
wet hair falling across her face.

"You could say that. I don't suppose you have a shoe
repair place in this town?" She looked at the bright red
heel in her hand.

Nate shook his head as he approached her. "Nope. But hand it over. I'll see what I can do."

A perfectly shaped brow arched high. "Why? Are you going to cobble them back together with—" she gestured around widely "—maybe some staples or screws?"

"Technically, what you just described is the definition of cobbling, so yeah. I've got some glue that'll do the trick." He met her gaze calmly. "It'd be a lot easier to do if you'd take the shoe off. Unless you also think I'm a blacksmith?"

He was teasing her. Something about this soaking-wet woman still having so much…regal bearing…amused Nate. He wasn't usually a fan of the pearl-clutching country club set who strutted through Gallant Lake on the weekends and referred to his family's hardware store as "adorable." But he couldn't help admiring this woman's ability to hold on to her superiority while looking like she accidentally went to a water park instead of the business meeting she was dressed for. To be honest, he also admired the figure that expensive red suit was clinging to as it dripped water on his floor.

He held out his hand. "I'm Nate Thomas. This is my store."

She let out an irritated sigh. "Brittany Doyle." She slid her long, slender hand into his and gripped with surprising strength. He held it for just a half second longer than necessary before shaking off the odd current of interest she invoked in him.

Don't miss
Changing His Plans *by Jo McNally,*
available September 2020 wherever
Harlequin Special Edition books and ebooks are sold.

Harlequin.com

Copyright © 2020 by Jo McNally

HSEEXP0820

Get 4 FREE REWARDS!

We'll send you 2 FREE Books <u>plus</u> 2 FREE Mystery Gifts.

Harlequin Special Edition books relate to finding comfort and strength in the support of loved ones and enjoying the journey no matter what life throws your way.

FREE
Value Over
$20

YES! Please send me 2 FREE Harlequin Special Edition novels and my 2 FREE gifts (gifts are worth about $10 retail). After receiving them, if I don't wish to receive any more books, I can return the shipping statement marked "cancel." If I don't cancel, I will receive 6 brand-new novels every month and be billed just $4.99 per book in the U.S. or $5.74 per book in Canada. That's a savings of at least 12% off the cover price! It's quite a bargain! Shipping and handling is just 50¢ per book in the U.S. and $1.25 per book in Canada.* I understand that accepting the 2 free books and gifts places me under no obligation to buy anything. I can always return a shipment and cancel at any time. The free books and gifts are mine to keep no matter what I decide.

235/335 HDN GNMP

Name (please print)

Address   Apt. #

City   State/Province   Zip/Postal Code

Email: Please check this box ☐ if you would like to receive newsletters and promotional emails from Harlequin Enterprises ULC and its affiliates. You can unsubscribe anytime.

Mail to the **Reader Service:**
IN U.S.A.: P.O. Box 1341, Buffalo, NY 14240-8531
IN CANADA: P.O. Box 603, Fort Erie, Ontario L2A 5X3

Want to try 2 free books from another series? Call 1-800-873-8635 or visit www.ReaderService.com.

---

*Terms and prices subject to change without notice. Prices do not include sales taxes, which will be charged (if applicable) based on your state or country of residence. Canadian residents will be charged applicable taxes. Offer not valid in Quebec. This offer is limited to one order per household. Books received may not be as shown. Not valid for current subscribers to Harlequin Special Edition books. All orders subject to approval. Credit or debit balances in a customer's account(s) may be offset by any other outstanding balance owed by or to the customer. Please allow 4 to 6 weeks for delivery. Offer available while quantities last.

Your Privacy—Your information is being collected by Harlequin Enterprises ULC, operating as Reader Service. For a complete summary of the information we collect, how we use this information and to whom it is disclosed, please visit our privacy notice located at corporate.harlequin.com/privacy-notice. From time to time we may also exchange your personal information with reputable third parties. If you wish to opt out of this sharing of your personal information, please visit readerservice.com/consumerschoice or call 1-800-873-8635. **Notice to California Residents**—Under California law, you have specific rights to control and access your data. For more information on these rights and how to exercise them, visit corporate.harlequin.com/california-privacy.

HSE20R2

New York Times bestselling author

RaeAnne Thayne

invites readers to return to Haven Point for
one last summer by the lake...

"RaeAnne Thayne gets better with every book."
—Robyn Carr, #1 *New York Times* bestselling author

Order your copy today!

HQNBooks.com

PHRTBPA0720

Love Harlequin romance?

DISCOVER.
Be the first to find out about promotions, news and exclusive content!

 Facebook.com/HarlequinBooks

Twitter.com/HarlequinBooks

Instagram.com/HarlequinBooks

Pinterest.com/HarlequinBooks

ReaderService.com

EXPLORE.
Sign up for the Harlequin e-newsletter and download a free book from any series at **TryHarlequin.com**

CONNECT.
Join our Harlequin community to share your thoughts and connect with other romance readers!
Facebook.com/groups/HarlequinConnection

 HARLEQUIN

HSOCIAL2020